THE POND

by

KEN FARMER

Cover Art by:
Ken Farmer

ISBN-13: 978-1-7363220-1-7

Timber Creek Press
Imprint of Timber Creek Productions, LLC
312 N. Commerce St.
Gainesville, Texas 76240

Published by: Timber Creek Press
timbercreekpresss@yahoo.com
www.timbercreekpress.net
Twitter: @pagact
Facebook Book Page:
www.facebook.com/TimberCreekPress
Ken's email: pagact@yahoo.com
214-533-4964

DEDICATION

This tome is dedicated to my favorite cousin, Frances Ann Magee Harrel of Shreveport, La. She is the inspiration for the character in the novel of Frances Ann.

ACKNOWLEDGMENT

The author gratefully acknowledges Lt. Colonel Clyde DeLoach, USMC (Ret.), T.C. Miller, Terry Heflin - retired English Professor at Tarrant County College, and best-selling author, Brad Dennison for their invaluable help in proofing, beta reading and editing this novel.

This novel is a work of fiction...except the parts that aren't. Names, characters, places, and incidents are either the products of the author's imagination or have been used fictitiously. Any resemblance to actual persons, living or dead, business establishments, events, or locales is entirely coincidental, except where they aren't.

TIMBER CREEK PRESS

CHAPTER ONE

THE POND

"Help! Help! Help me, Foot! Help me!" Hutch thrashed about in the clear, but dark water of Unka Dud's spring fed pond. He was only 'bout ten or twelve feet from the bank.

His nappy head went under, then came back up as he sputtered an' cried out again.

I dove in, swam to him, grabbed one of his flailin' hands an' pulled him back in the shallows where he could touch bottom so we could walk up to the bank.

Tiny, my smallish orange and white fox terrier-whippit cross was there, dancin' around waitin' for me to come back out of the water.

We called this pond deep in the woods, Unka Dud's Pond. 'Course he wadn't nobody's uncle that we know 'bout, least not around here, but heard he's a nice man 'bout Mister Tom's age, maybe a bit older, with a funny accent—but he lets us swim an' fish whenever we want to.

Pond's been here a really long time. It's spring fed, deep as a tree an' looks black. But that's only 'cause it's real clear but there's a passel of moss an' algae an' stuff on the bottom that makes it look black—cold as the dickens, even in the summer. Kinda looks like some prehistoric monster creature might live here.

It was gettin' close to fall an' school was startin' soon. Trees'll be turnin' in a month or so.

"Didn't know you couldn't swim, Hutch. Good thing daddy ain't here, he'd throw your black butt back in out yonder." I pointed out toward the middle of the pond. "That's what he did to me last year over at Three Creeks. Threw me out in the middle an' made me swim to him...It was either that or drown."

"Aw, he wouldn't't'ove let you drown...would he?"

"Well, probably not, but he made me think so at the time...That's when I stepped on that girl Bethany's body on the bottom."

"I kicked somethin' hard an' round when I first walked off in that deep hole...It was on the bottom, too."

"What was it?"

"How the heck do I know? Was more concerned with gettin' my face back above the surface so I could breathe...How'd you learn to swim so good if you just learned when he chunked you out in the creek last summer?"

"Well, actually, kinda liked it, so when we went back to Gainesville after daddy's vacation was over, I talked mama into enrollin' me in the free Red Cross classes they had down to the city pool...Took lessons all the rest of the summer. Don't take long to learn once you start if you ain't scared...an' daddy's little trick took care of that."

"Wow, they don't even have a pool at Junction City."

"Well, think I can teach you...just gotta trust me, though."

"Oh, boy. You have this habit of gettin' us in trouble when you say that."

"Do not."

"Do too."

"Do not."

"Do too."

"Where'd you kick that hard round thing?"

"Huh? Where'd that come from? Thought we were talkin' 'bout you gettin' us in trouble."

"No, you were...Now, where'd you hit that thing?"

"There's a drop off hole 'bout ten feet or so out there where I was. The dang bottom just fell out from under me."

"Okay."

I took a big breath, dove into the water 'bout where I figured he'd been, ducked down under the surface an' swam to the bottom. Felt like 'bout eight or nine feet—wadn't hard. Could see a little bit. Started feelin' 'round an' sure 'nuff, felt of somethin' hard an' round. I grabbed a hold an' swam back to the surface an' to the shallows where I could stand. It wadn't very heavy.

Tiny had her front paws in the water waitin' for me.

I looked down at what I had in my hand. "Aiiii!" I dropped it back in the water.

"What was it?"

I looked up at him. "A skull."

"What kinda skull?"

"What kinds are there?"

"Animal, people...You know?"

"Oh, right...It was a people skull."

"What'd you drop it for?"

"Well, it scared me."

"Did it look at you or talk to you...bite you?"

"Uh...no."

He shook his head an' shrugged his shoulders. "Well?"

I frowned, took a breath an went back under, picked up the thing, an' walked out to the bank. I set it on the ground. Tiny cautiously tiptoed up an' sniffed, then lowered herself down a bit an' barked a couple times at it.

The hollow eyes looked up at us an' the jaw was kinda open like it was grinnin' or somethin'.

"Yep, that's a people skull awright...Wow! Look at those holes in the middle of the forehead."

"Huh..." I stuck my finger in one, they were side-by-side. "Bet a quarter they're bullet holes."

"You think?"

"Uh-huh. We'll take it to grandpa, he'll know for sure."

"Think there's anymore down there?"

"Maybe. I'll dive down there again next time we come back." I looked up at the sky an' the sun was already behind the thick, tall trees to the west. "We best get a wiggle on toward the house. Don't do to be late to grandma's supper."

"Got that right."

I put the thing under my arm, like I was totin' a football. We made our way along the narrow trail through the woods in the direction of grandpa's fence on the south side of his place.

It was purtnear a quarter mile through the piney woods that had some hickory, pecan, sweet gum an' black gum mixed it. Tiny ran through the trees sniffin' for coon scat or squirrel trails.

Got fussed at by some fox an' gray squirrels along the way for disturbin' their food gatherin' for the comin' winter, which was in full swing.

THE POND

"You know where Unka Dud lives?"

"Never been there, but Don an' them told me it was on past the pond a ways…Purty secluded, they said. Can get to it by a old loggin' road from the other side."

"Ever met 'im?"

"Uh-uh. They said he was 'bout Mister Tom's age or older an' talked funny, though."

"Funny ha-ha or funny, odd?"

"Like a foreigner."

"What kinda foreigner?"

"Well, how do I know. Never talked to him…Geemanie whilikers, Hutch, some of your questions are really dumb sometimes."

"They're only dumb 'cause you can't answer 'em."

"Don't remember takin' you to raise."

"Ha, wouldn't know how anyways."

"Would too."

"Would not."

I thumped his shoulder an' he thumped me back. Dang good thing we liked each other.

I held the second wire of grandpa's fence up an' put my foot on the third one so he could crawl through. Then he did the same from the other side so I could. Too easy to hang a pant leg or your butt if there wadn't somebody holdin' the bob wire outta the way while Tiny scooted under the bottom one.

Another ten minutes got us through the pasture an' up to the gate that led to grandma an' grandpa's big ol' house. Think it was built back durin' the 1800s sometime. Don't believe it'd been painted since then.

Tiny ran on up to the picket fence, jumped it, which wadn't hard for her. We wadn't 'bout to try it, so we went through the gate in the middle an' walked up the flagstone pathway to the front porch an' climbed the stoop.

Wadn't nobody on the porch, so we went on inside, down the big wide hallway, called a dog run. Musta been twelve feet or so wide. Grandma had couches, chairs an' little tables 'long the sides . Grandma's kitchen was at the end on the left side. The whole house had twelve or thirteen foot ceilin's, guess so's the heat could rise an' be carried out the screen doors at the front an' back. Ever room had these transom things that opened

THE POND

above all the doors for the ventilation. Never was too hot inside, even durin' the middle of the summer.

As usual, grandma was in the kitchen, cookin' on her big cast wood iron cook stove. That sucker could put out some heat, too. Grandma wouldn't weigh a hunderd pounds soakin' wet an' I never saw her break a sweat standin' over that thing.

They didn't have electricity out there yet. We did where we lived in Junction City, though. Daddy had been transferred here from Gainesville, Texas, durin' the winter. There was a bunch of oil drillin' goin' on—he was a driller for Shell Oil.

She looked up from stirrin' the pot of butter beans when we walked in. "What's that you're carrying there, Foot?"

I held the skull out so she could see. Grandma screeched like draggin' a chair across a hardwood floor, dropped her wooden spoon on the linoleum, an' put her hand to her chest.

"Oh, my Lord have mercy, take that...that out of my kitchen, Foot."

She bent over, picked up her spoon an' pointed toward the door with it. "Lord, Lord, Lord, you

13

boys will be the death of me yet...Now scat and take that thing outside."

Me, Hutch, an' Tiny headed back to the front door.

"Guess you crapped an' fell back in it this time, Foot."

"Wadn't thinkin' it'd scare her."

"Uh-huh."

Grandpa was sittin' on the stoop when we went back out, takin' off his ankle-high brogans. Grandma didn't allow him to come inside wearin' his workin' boots—tracks in too much sand. She'd peel his head like an' onion.

He looked up when the screen door slammed behind him. "Whatcha got, boys...Good goshamighty...Where'd you get that?"

"Unka Dud's pond, Grandpa. It was on the bottom 'bout ten or twelve feet from the bank." I held it out to him.

He took it, turned it over in his hands, an' then studied the holes in the front.

"Hmm, bullet holes...two of them."

"How old do you think that is, Grandpa?"

"Found it underwater, you say?"

"Uh-huh."

THE POND

"Have to get Doc Duckworth to take a look, but I'm going to say forty, maybe fifty years…give or take." He looked up at us again. "No question, boys, whoever this was…was murdered."

§§§

CHAPTER TWO

JOLLEY'S STORE

Grandpa, me, an' Hutch walked the couple hunderd yards over toward the Haynesville Road an' Smead Jolley's store. He had a slogan on a sign 'bove the front screen door. - 'If we don't have it, you don't need it'. Grandpa an' Smead were cousins or somethin' like that.

THE POND

Tiny went with us, like she usually does. 'Sides, didn't want her to haul off that skull an' go to gnawin' on it. Seen her eyein' it while we were out on the porch—can't keep a dog from bein' a dog.

Cousin Smead had played in the majors for the Chicago White Sox an' grandpa told me he was the only player in major league history to make three errors on one play. Not sure I'd want that kinda record.

Grandpa got us a RC cocola apiece while he borrowed Cousin Smead's telephone in the store.

"Don't tell your grandma, she'll accuse me of spoilin' your supper."

We both drew our fingers across our mouths like a zipper.

Cousin Smead had the only phone around, not to say nothin' 'bout electricity. The co-op said they'd be runnin' power lines over to grandpa's house next year, or so. Grandpa said he wadn't holdin' his breath.

Cousin Smead gave Tiny a little chunk of hog's head cheese from the glass case he kept cold cuts, cheese, slab bacon, an' stuff in. You could get a big ol' ham, roast beef, or salami sandwich, or just some cheese, crackers, viennie sausage, an' a pickle for lunch there, if you wanted.

I could hear grandpa talkin' to Sheriff Wilson.

"Myron, if you're gonna be out this way, need you to come by. Foot an' Hutch found a skull in Dud's Pond...got what looks to me like a couple of bullet holes in it...Might want to bring Doc Duckworth. 'Magine he'll want to take a gander, too...Uh-huh, that's right...said bullet holes."

Grandpa nodded his head. Don't know why, 'cause the sheriff couldn't see 'im.

"Yeah...Chicken'ndumplin's, think...Uh-huh, figured...Okay, I'll tell Mame...Laterbye."

He hung up the receiver thing on the side of the phone on the wall an' turned to us. "The sheriff'll bring Doc Duckworth with him. Gotta go tell Mame to set two more plates for supper."

"What's this about a skull with bullet holes, John?"

Grandpa looked at Cousin Smead an' nodded. "Yep, Foot an' Hutch found a skull with a couple of what looks like bullet holes in the forehead in Dud's...keep it quiet, though."

Cousin Smead chuckled. "What for? You know Mabel at the switchboard in El Dorado listens in on every call to the sheriff's station. Gonna be all over the county by in the mornin'."

Grandpa grimaced. "Oh, damn, forgot about Mabel...You're right, Smead. Like takin' an ad out in the newspaper."

Me an' Hutch finished our RCs an' sold the bottles back to Cousin Smead for two cents each. We put 'em in a wood case he kept beside the cooler an' our two zinc pennies in our pockets. They made a bunch of zinc pennies durin' the war so they could use the copper for ammo casings an' stuff.

We caught up with grandpa purty quick. He was walkin' with Mister Tom who was carryin' a half bushel basket of pears to grandma.

"You boys carry this basket for Tom. He's toted it all the way from his house...near a mile."

"Yessir."

Mister Tom set the basket in the road, shook his hands an' flexed his fingers. Tiny sniffed of the pears an' decided they weren't for her.

Me an' Hutch got on each side of the basket an' grabbed the wire handles. Half bushel of pears is fair heavy. They were those big round ones, kinda shaped like apples, called summer pears—they're really sweet, crisp, an' juicy.

Grandma makes preserves out of 'em—the ones we don't eat first, that is. Reckon she'll set one more plate at the table. When she makes chicken'ndumplin's, she makes a bunch.

People seem to know when she makes 'em—kinda spooky, actually.

Mister Tom looked at grandpa. "A skull you say?"

"Yep, two bullet holes almost in the center just above the left eye."

We walked into the yard.

"Take those pears on back to your grandma."

I nodded. "Yessir."

Grandpa stepped over to the small table on the porch where he had set the skull. He picked it up an' handed it to Mister Tom.

Me an' Hutch hustled down the dog run to the kitchen with the basket.

"Here's some summer pears Mister Tom brought over, Grandma."

"Oh, good, I'll make some preserves tomorrow. Set them in the pantry."

THE POND

We did what she said, then ran back down the hall. Wanted to hear what Mister Tom had to say about the skull.

"Well, believe you're right, John...bullet holes. I'd say .38 caliber or 9 millimeter...hard to tell."

He turned the skull over. "Didn't go through."

Mister Tom shook it. There was a rattle. He looked at grandpa.

"May be one left inside...Hold your hand under the brain stem hole."

He listened real close as the object rolled across the inside while he slowly turned the skull—somethin' fell out the hole in the bottom into grandpa's hand.

"Yep, a bullet." Grandpa held it up between his thumb and finger.

Mister Tom set the skull back down on the small table, took the bullet from grandpa, studied it a few seconds, an' nodded. "I'm going to say, this is a 7.65 millimeter...Nose is flattened, but bet a dollar it's a 7.65."

He looked at grandpa, then out at the front where Sheriff Wilson's dark green Buick pulled up an' parked under the sycamore trees.

The sheriff an' Doc Duckworth got out an' headed toward the house.

Sheriff Wilson noticed the skull in Mister Tom's hands. "Well, all we need now are some cross bones and we could call a meetin' of the Skull an' Cross Bones club."

Me an' Hutch glanced at one another.

I nodded at 'im. "If there ain't a Skull an' Cross Bones club, there oughta be."

"Yeah...Sounds neat. Maybe we oughta start one."

They climbed the steps to the porch an' everbody shook hands like they always do. Don't know why they just don't say 'hidy' an' be done with it, but they don't.

Doctor Duckworth pointed at the skull on the table. "Let's see what we have there, Tom."

Mister Tom picked the skull back up and handed it to the doc. He took the skull, looked at the holes, then turned it all around an' nodded. "Agree, bullet holes, John."

"Tom think's they're 7.65 millimeter."

The doctor looked at Mister Tom. "7.65 millimeter. What in the world?"

THE POND

"My WWI German Luger fires a 7.65 millimeter, but most of the ones in WWII were 9 millimeter."

"Do you have any idea how old it might be, Doc?"

He looked at me an' Hutch. "Say you found it at the bottom of Dud's pond?"

"Yessir...Nine, ten feet down."

"That's a spring fed lake, isn't it?"

Me an' Hutch both nodded.

He looked at grandpa, the sheriff, an' Mister Tom. "Considering the fact that it's spring fed and that deep, going to be pretty cold down there and very little oxygen to stimulate the oxidation...Bone's not going to degrade very fast."

"Yessir...was right cold."

"Well, with a by gosh an' by golly...going to say thirty-five years, or more." He scraped the surface of the skull with his thumb nail. "Well stained with algae an' moss...Any more bones down there, Foot?"

"Don't know, sir, didn't look no more after findin' the skull."

He looked at the sheriff. "I'd say need to search for the rest of the skeleton, Myron."

"I figured on doin' that very thing, Doctor Duckworth...tomorra."

"Sun was already past the trees when Foot pulled that thing out. Plus didn't want to be late for supper," added Hutch.

"Reckon we need to go back out there with you, Foot."

"I can dive too."

The sheriff looked at Mister Tom. "Wouldn't hurt to have a couple divers down there lookin', thanks." He turned to grandpa. "What do you know about this Dud fella, John?"

"My understanding is his real name's Eric Hoffer, accordin' to my daddy...just goes by Dud."

"Any idea what he does for a living?"

Grandpa shook his head. "None...Always seems to have enough money to live on an' pay his property taxes, though."

"How long has he lived there, John?"

Grandpa kinda shrugged. "Been back there in the woods since I was about twenty-one or maybe twenty-two, Myron...Think he was about thirty or so when he moved here. Makes him in his mid 60s now...Always kept to his self."

THE POND

Mister Tom looked at the sheriff. "That would have been around the start of WWI."

§§§

CHAPTER THREE

THE POND

It was 'bout eleven o'clock when we headed out toward Unka Dud's pond from the house. Wanted to wait till the sun was high so there would be more light down under that dark water—plus it was 'bout ninety-five degrees which would help 'cause it was goin' to be cold as the dickens nine-ten feet deep.

THE POND

Grandpa had used one of those tall bicycle pumps to air up a big ol' caisson inner tube from his two-ton truck so we could tie a tow sack in the center. We'd float it out over where we were divin' so we didn't have to go to the bank ever time we found a bone—not sayin' nothin' 'bout somethin' to grab hold of to rest out there. Guess we'll hang a rock from it to anchor it in place.

Mister Tom carried a thermos of hot coffee grandma had fixed to warm us up with. Now, I ain't real high on black coffee to begin with, but I've drunk it with daddy a time or two when I went out to his rig with him. It's like he always says, 'Ain't no hill for a stepper'.

Hutch carried two blankets for when me an' Mister Tom come out of that water. Figure we could be a mite cold. I took one from him so he didn't have to carry both.

Sheriff Wilson an' Doc Duckworth weren't totin' nothin'—guess 'cause they was the oldest. Well, the doctor was carryin' his black bag. Hope he didn't need it.

It was kind of a process goin' through grandpa's back fence, what with the transferrin' of all the stuff an' the holdin' of the bob wire so everbody could crawl through. But we got 'er done. Tiny ducked under the bottom one, as usual.

We worked our way along the trail through the woods to the pond. Think the same squirrels that fussed at me an' Hutch was fussin' at the bunch of us again as we passed goin' back. Sure didn't like their nut gatherin' bein' interrupted.

Doctor Duckworth looked at the dark water an' the tall trees that surrounded it when we walked out of the trees. "Goodness, even looks spooky. Wouldn't be surprised to see some prehistoric monster come out of that water."

Sheriff Wilson looked at me when we walked up to the edge of the pond. "Point to the spot where you found the skull, Foot."

"Right yonder, 'bout ten, twelve yards out there, just past a drop-off that Hutch stepped in." I aimed my finger out a ways from the bank toward the area.

Me an' Mister Tom got ready to go in the water. After takin' his shoes an' socks off, then his shirt, he pulled his Luger an' his billfold out of his pocket an' handed 'em to the sheriff.

THE POND

I didn't have to do nothin' but take my yo-yo an' Barlow jack knife out of my pockets an' give 'em to Hutch—I was ready to go.

Grandpa found a rock to tie to the inner tube 'long with the tow sack. He set 'em in the water next to the edge of the bank.

Mister Tom waded in, grabbed the float an' rock, then turned to me. "Lead the way, Foot."

I waded out past him till I got to the drop-off an' turned 'round to him. "Falls off right here."

He towed the inner tube out, feelin' 'long with his foot when he got close till he found the edge. An' that's where he measured out an' tied off the rope holdin' the rock, then dropped it right there. The tow sack was hangin' down with the top open in the center.

Mister Tom looked at me an' nodded. We both took several deep breaths, ducked under the water an' swam to the bottom.

Little over halfway down we hit what almost felt like a wall where the water suddenly turned downright cold all the rest of the way to the bottom. Found out later that wall or layer is called a *thermocline*.

Could see a little bit down there 'cause the sun was almost overhead an' shinin' straight down—even though it was kinda like lookin' through green tinted blurry glass. There was only shade on the lake where branches stuck out over the water.

I felt of somethin' that was 'round eighteen inches long an' hard, there was also two other pieces together at the end. I picked them up, too, an' headed to the surface.

Looked like some kinda leg bones to me, so I dropped them in the tow sack in the inner tube. Held on to a rope grandpa had wrapped 'round the tube for that purpose an' took some more deep breaths.

Mister Tom came to the surface while I was breathin'. He had a whole string of bones I figured was the backbone. Looked a lot like what come out of a deer or cow. He put 'em in the sack an' started doin' what I was, storin' up air to go back down—could stay longer'n me, guess 'cause he was older.

Took one more breath an' ducked back under. I could stay down there 'bout thirty or forty-five seconds. Found several more pieces, didn't know what they were, but brought 'em up anyway. Mister Tom was already gone.

My next trip, got what I figured was a bunch of rib bones an' dropped them in the sack. He come up with what looked like a passel of fingers or toes an' put them in the sack while I was duckin' back under.

I was steady feelin' 'round on the bottom an' for some reason, I looked up. Not a foot in front of my face was the big old beak of a snappin' turtle. His head musta been bigger'n one of grandpa's cantaloupes.

Didn't know you could scream under water—but I'm here to say you dang sure can. I shot to the surface fast as I could while that big sucker just turned an' swam off. Shell was near big around as a washtub.

Grandpa says that if a snappin' turtle bites you, he'll hang on till sundown. Wadn't real anxious to find out if that was right.

Mister Tom come up right after I hit the surface. He looked at me an' noticed my eyes were big as saucers.

"What's the matter, Foot?"

"Snap...snappin' turtle." I turned lose of the tube an' held up my hands wide for a second. "This big."

"Dang, that's a big one. Guess he swam off. Probably scared him as much as he did you."

I shook my head. "Hope he knows that."

We went on searchin' for a while. Never knew the body had that many bones in it. Figured it was goin' to be hard to tell when we got 'em all.

Me an' Mister Tom come up once at the same time. He looked at me while we was droppin' more bones in the sack an' laughed.

I frowned at him. "What's funny?"

He grinned big. "Looks like you been eatin' muskadine grapes. Your lips are blue."

I rubbed my mouth. "You mean like yours?"

"Probably...We should go to the bank an' warm up, before continuing. What say?"

My teeth were chatterin' as I nodded.

He pulled the inner tube over 'bout a foot where he could stand on the bottom, unhooked the sack, an' drug it out the bank. Doctor Duckworth took it, pulled it on up higher an' dumped out.

THE POND

A whole rafter of green bones fell out an' one water-soaked stick.

We waded up out of the water—both of us were shivering an' had our arms wrapped around our chests. Grandpa an' the sheriff quickly draped a blanket around our shoulders while Hutch poured us each hot coffee in some cups we had brought along.

Me an' Mister Tom both squatted down with our blankets wrapped 'round us an' holdin' those cups in both hands. The heat comin' from it sure felt good—an' the first sip was real warmin', didn't notice the bitter atall.

Quit shakin' in a few minutes an' drinkin' most of the cup of coffee. Mister Tom looked at me. "Say when you're ready, Foot."

I nodded. "Give me a couple more minutes, Mister Tom."

He grinned. "I'm for that."

Doctor Duckworth was layin' out the bones in some kinda order he seemed to know 'bout while grandpa kept shooin' Tiny away. Think she thought those bones were for her.

'Bout the time me an' Mister Tom had warmed up some, the doc had those bones laid out where you could tell they actually had been a person at one time.

He stood, looked down at his handy work, an' rubbed his chin. "Going to say this fellow was fairly close to six feet...give or take a couple of inches."

The sheriff pointed. "Did he break his left arm at one time?"

Doctor Duckworth nodded. "Probably as a teenager."

Grandpa glanced over at the skeleton. "Any guess as to how old he was?"

The doc mashed his lips together. "I'd say in his late twenties to early thirties...Not a lot of wear on the joints."

Mister Tom got to his feet. "What are we missin'?"

Doctor Duckworth puffed his cheeks then blew his breath out. "Some foot and hand phelangies, left clavicle, right patella, an' left scapula, plus three cervicals."

'Course I had no clue what he was talkin' 'bout 'cept the hand an' foot part—just some more bones down there.

THE POND

The doc studied the bones a few more minutes. "Uh-oh."

The sheriff's head snapped up. "Hate it when a doctor says 'uh-oh'…What is it, Ralph? Spit it out."

"Just noticed…" He turned to look at the sheriff and frowned. "Got two right calcaneus."

"English, you old quack."

The doc lifted his eyebrow. "Heel bones…Myron. We have two right heel bones."

The sheriff looked at the pond over his shoulder. "Oh, damn." He turned back to me an' Mister Tom. "Gotta spread your search, boys…there's another one down there."

§§§

CHAPTER FOUR

THE POND

Mister Tom moved the inner tube out 'bout another ten feet. We dove down where we had been lookin', an' then moved out a bit to start feelin' 'round. Brrr, cold again.

I found what I took to be the hip bones, swam back up an' dropped the kinda large piece in the sack.

THE POND

Mister Tom came up just as I dove back down. Could see he had some more bones, too. When I got to the bottom I found the skull right off. Even had a couple of the neck bones still hooked on.

Dropped it in the sack after swimmin' back to the top and held on to the tube for a minute while I took more deep breaths.

Mister Tom came back up with double handfuls of more bones. Guess we found the mother load. Heard a gold miner character say that in a Hopalong Cassidy movie, *Hidden Gold*, one time at the pitchur show.

'Bout thirty minutes later, Mister Tom an' me were both blue again with our teeth chatterin' when we came up with what we hoped was a final load.

He looked over at me. "Think we've p…pretty well got it, slick…You ha…had enough?"

I just nodded. My mouth wouldn't work.

He pulled up the anchor rock an' kicked over to the shallower water where he could stand. I just swam as best I could toward the bank, an' then walked out.

Felt like a walkin' icicle. Guess grandpa thought I looked like one as he quickly wrapped a blanket 'round me.

"Cold, Foot?"

I nodded an' managed to squeak out a, "Y…y…yessir…a little."

They had built a fire back up the bank a ways an' I headed straight for it. Hutch brought me a cup of hot coffee.

The sheriff helped Mister Tom out, an' then drug the tube up on the bank with the sack full of bones. Doc Duckworth unhooked it an' dumped the bones out over next to the other bunch. He picked up the skull, first thing.

I was holdin' the cup in both hands, feelin' the warmth of it while I took sips an' watched the doc study the skull. Finally he looked over at grandpa, the sheriff, an' Mister Tom.

He held the skull up. "Two bullet holes in this one, too. Close to the same place…Like the first one, these are a little jagged which tells me they were shot at very close range." He looked up an' nodded. "Another murder…both execution style."

Hutch's mouth dropped open. "Gol-uh-olee!"

"About the same age, doc?"

THE POND

"Bit older, I'd say, John...Maybe ten years or so. More wear on the teeth."

"Think the bullets are still inside?"

The doc glanced at Mister Tom who had joined me at the fire with his own cup of coffee.

He shook the skull—there was a rattle.

"Sounds like it."

The doc slowly turned the skull over, held it up above his head an' rotated it, lookin' up the hole in the bottom, kinda like tryin' to get a quarter out of a piggy bank. In just a couple of turns, somethin' fell out—a bullet, then another one. There was two inside this skull.

The sheriff bent over an' picked the flattened bullets up an' looked at 'em in the palm of his hand. Mister Tom stepped up to see 'em—still had his blanket wrapped around his shoulders like me. His lips weren't blue anymore.

He reached out an' took one from the sheriff's hand an' rolled it between his thumb an' first finger. "Believe these are the same caliber as the other...7.65 millimeter."

The sheriff turned to the doc. "Think you got any more extra bones this time, Ralph?"

He shook his head. "Doesn't appear so, Myron...Unless there's another set in a different part of the pond."

Sheriff Wilson ground his teeth together an' looked out over the water. "No way of knowin' without scourin' the whole damn lake." He looked at grandpa. "What do you think, John, about three, four acres?"

"At least, Myron. Maybe a tad more...Just puredee luck the boys stumbled across these."

UNION COUNTY SHERIFF'S OFFICE

The Union County Sheriff's department was located in the first floor of the court house in downtown El Dorado, Arkansas.

Two blond-haired men in tailored suits and gray fedoras stood in front of the reception desk in the outer office, their hats in their hands. Both blue-eyed men were in their forties.

"Deputy, ve'd like to speak to ze sheriff, is he in?"

Deputy Clarence Walker looked up. "What's this about?"

THE POND

The two exchanged glances.

"Vell, ve'd just like to speak mit him."

Walker leaned back in his chair and studied the two strangers.

"Ya'll're not from around here, I take it?"

Again the glances.

"Uh...*Nein*, ve are Dutch, from...Amsterdam."

"Amsterdam?"

"*Ja.*"

"Where's that?"

"Ze Netherlands."

The deputy frowned. "Is that Holland?"

Both men rolled their eyes a little.

"*Ja*, Holland."

Walker leaned over his desk to look at their feet. "Don't wear wooden shoes, huh?"

Both men got a confused looked on their face, then finally the man that hadn't said anything spoke up, "Oh, ve only wear zose at home." He had a slight grin on his face.

"Ah, makes sense."

"May ve see ze sheriff now?"

"Well, he ain't here."

Again the eye rolls.

The first man spoke again, "And vere could ve find ze sheriff?"

"Him an' Doc Duckworth are out to Big John Jamison's place…seein' 'bout a murder."

"Vere is zis Big Yon Yamison's place?"

Walker shook his head. "No, it's Big John Jamison."

The man frowned. "*Ja*, vhat I said, Big Yon Yamison."

It was Deputy Walker's turn to roll his eyes. "It's out the Haynesville Road 'bout 18 miles. Right behind Jolley's Store."

"Vere is zis…Haynesville Rrrroad?"

Deputy Walker took a breath and blew it out. "That'd be county road 15." He pointed. "Turn left from the court house an' git on Robert E. Lee Street an' just stay on it…Becomes Haynesville Road." He looked back down at his paperwork indicating he was finished with the conversation.

"*Danke* for ze information, Deputy."

He didn't look up as the two men turned and headed to the door. "Uh-huh."

When the man closed the door behind them, Walker cocked his head, then looked up at the door. "Donkey?…What in hell?"

THE POND

THE POND

Grandpa pulled another tow sack hangin' from his back pocket. "Good thing I thought to bring an extra sack." He handed it to Doctor Duckworth.

"Glad you did too, John. Hate to mix all these bones up…take forever to get them segregated again." The doc started sackin' up the first set.

Grandpa turned to me an' Mister Tom. "Ya'll about to get warmed up?"

"Gettin' there, Grandpa. Gettin' there." I held my hands out to the fire—the blanket hung over my shoulders an' was draggin' the ground behind me.

Mister Tom pulled his gray sweatshirt over his head, then sat down on the ground an' put on his socks an' shoes.

"These pants will dry by the time we get back to John's house, Foot…Day's warming up nicely."

We took a few more minutes standin' close to the fire, first with our fronts, then we'd turn around to warm up our backsides.

The birds, squirrels, an' bugs I guess had got used to us bein' there, 'cause they were all chatterin', singin', an' buzzin' again. There was even a occasional fish slappin' the top of the water out in the middle of the pond.

Grandpa looked at me. "When is your daddy's days off, Foot?"

"He gets Saturday an' Sunday this week."

"Oughta get JB, Don, an' Hubert an' go fishing over at Lock 7 on the Ouachita. Channel cat should be bitin'. I'm 'bout ready for a fish fry...Ya'll?"

"Sounds like a capital idea, John. Could use a break."

Doctor Duckworth glanced over at the sheriff. "From what? You don't do anything, but strut around trying to look important."

"You should talk, you damned old quack. My leg still hurts from that botched up job you did diggin' that bullet out last year the Cobb boy put in it."

"Not my fault you didn't have the sense to stay off of it...like I told you to."

Folks that didn't know would think those two hated each other. Truth is, they'd been best friends since high school. Neither one would admit it, though. Think they just enjoyed pokin' at one another. Sometimes it was like watchin' Abbott an' Costello.

"All right, got these bones all sacked backed up." He handed one tow sack to the sheriff. "Here, Wyatt Earp, you can make yourself useful and carry one."

"Figured I would have to do your job for you." He took the bag.

Grandpa untied the rock from the caisson inner tube an' grabbed one of the ropes tied around to hold it. Me an' Mister Tom carried our damp blankets while Hutch toted the empty thermos. Grandpa kicked dirt over what was left of the fire an' we headed to the path that led to his fence.

Nobody noticed a set of brown eyes watchin' us leave from the brush on the other side of the pond at the time—'cept maybe Tiny. She kept lookin' back over her shoulder at the pond.

§§§

CHAPTER FIVE

JAMISON HOME

We walked up to the house after closin' the pasture gate behind us. There was one of those white Stanley Coffee van trucks parked out front.

They went around to folks out in the country, 'specially those that lived quite a ways from town, sellin' 'em things they might need. Had coffee, of course, an' other stuff, salt, sugar, pots, pans, cannin' supplies, an' what have you. They even made that thermos we took down to the pond for the coffee. Daddy had one he carried to work, too.

Grandma looked forward to them comin' by 'cause she was always needin' somethin'. She even got her little tins of Garrett snuff that she kept hidden in her dress. Said she was buyin' snuff for grandpa, but she always slipped some for herself—thought nobody knew, but we all did anyway.

The salesman was on the porch, tippin' his hat to grandma when we came through the gate. The sheriff an' Doc Duckworth stopped an' put the tow sacks of bones in the trunk of his car—all but the first skull which was still sittin' on the little table up on the porch.

She looked up as we walked toward the stoop. "Anybody needs anything, better speak up while Clyde's here, won't be back for two or three weeks."

Mister Tom glanced up at him. "Could use a couple tins of coffee, if you don't mind?"

"Sure, Mister Rayford, saves me a trip over to your place. Think that's all you'll need this time?"

Everbody 'round knew Mister Tom on account he had been given the Medal of Honor for stuff he did in World War I over in France against the Germans when he was in the Marine Corps. They called the Marines, 'Devil Dogs'. He was a honest to gosh American hero.

"Well, wouldn't hurt to get a can of lard while you're here."

"Easy enough."

The Stanley Coffee man went out to his Chevy panel van, got the coffee an' lard an' brought it back in the yard for Mister Tom.

He handed him a couple dollars an' the salesman gave him a quarter back.

The Stanley man looked a bit confused. "These bills are a little damp. Fall in the creek or somethin', Tom?"

"Something like that." Mister Tom grinned. "Can't do without my coffee. Lived on it in the Corps.

The salesman tipped his hat again. "See ya'll in a few weeks, then. Appreciate your business."

Grandma nodded. "Glad you came by, Clyde. I was needing some things…Enjoy those cookies."

THE POND

"I fully intend to Miz Jamison. Sure smell good…an' thank you." He waved as he got in his van an' drove off to Unka JB's just a hunderd yards down the road. Aunt Thelma usually always needed somethin', too.

"You got cookies, Grandma?"

"Just happen to have a fresh batch of oatmeal raisin, Foot. You and Hutch don't want any, do you?"

Hutch had a grin on his face that went from side to side. "Sure don't have to ask us twice, Miz Jamison, nosireebob, sure don't." He looked at me. "Ain't that right, Foot?"

"Uh-huh."

Tiny heard the word 'cookie' an' went to spinnin' 'round—she loved cookies, too.

Grandma turned an' grabbed the screen door handle. "You boys wait right there, your feet are dirty. I'll bring some out with a glass of buttermilk each."

"Okay, Grandma."

Me an' Hutch elbowed each other an' sat down on the edge of the porch, lettin' our feet hang down to wait on our cookies.

A fairly new black Ford pulled up out under the sycamores an' two men in suits got out. They came through the gate an' walked up to where we all were on the porch. Both of 'em took their hats off—coulda been brothers, I guess, 'cause both had kinda blond hair.

They looked at the sheriff—guess they knew it was him on account he was wearin' his khaki uniform with his badge pinned on the front an' a light gray Stetson.

"Sheriff Vilson?"

He nodded. "I am and ya'll are?"

The one standin' sorta to the front looked at the other feller. "Zis is Elias Vebber an' I'm Jonas Becker. Ze deputy at ze office gave us directions vhere you were."

"Wonderful."

"Ve're seekin' ze...friend from back home, a Motshan Bieler. Ve hoped you might know of hem."

They sure talked funny—sounded almost like a machine gun rattlin' words off. All of 'em were fast an' chopped off—almost hard to understand. Must be foreigners.

THE POND

Me an' Hutch looked at each other. Funny thing was, Mister Tom had his head cocked to the side an' one eyebrow was kinda raised.

The sheriff, grandpa, Doc, an' Mister Tom all exchanged glances an' shook their heads.

"Don't believe any of us ever heard that name around here.

The two men looked at one another.

"Maybe he goes by different name. Vould zound German...or Dutch."

The sheriff shook his head again. "Can't help you. Doesn't fit anybody I know."

The second fella's eyes fell on the skull sittin' on the table behind grandpa. They kinda went big.

The first feller glanced at his friend. "Vell, ve had heard he moved to zis area before ze var."

Mister Tom spoke up, "Which war?"

"Oh...ze Great Var, of course."

"Ah, World War I..."

"*Ja...ja.* Ze First Vorld Var."

Both men replaced their fedoras, nodded an' turned around.

"*Danke.*"

Mister Tom had a slight smile. "*Bitte schoen.*"

The two men both had a little start, dipped their heads an' walked back to their car.

Hutch leaned over to me. "Wonder what donkey means? Don't think they were talkin' 'bout a jackass."

"Mister Tom must know. He answered 'em with that bitte shown word."

They started up an' drove back off toward the Haynesville Road.

Sheriff Wilson opened his mouth to ask Mister Tom a question, but I reckon I musta beat him to it.

"What does that donkey an' bitte shown mean, Mister Tom?"

He glanced at me. "Thank you and you're welcome, Foot…in German."

Grandpa nodded. "Thought that was a German accent. Same way Eric Hoffer talks, but a lot faster."

Hutch looked at me funny.

"Unka Dud."

"Oh."

"Sheriff Wilson."

He looked at me. "What is it, Foot?"

"Noticed that one feller that wadn't doin' much talkin' was sure interested in that skull." I pointed over on the table.

He turned around an' looked at it. "Huh, forgot that was still there."

The doc stepped over an' picked it up. "Guess I better add it to the rest of the bones."

Mister Tom ran his fingers through his hair. "That name of the man they said they were looking for…Motshan Bieler…is Jewish German."

"They said he came over here before WWI." The sheriff looked at Mister Tom. "I didn't think the Jews were getting persecuted over there till right before WWII an' the rise of Adolph Hitler and the Nazis."

Mister Tom shook his head. "The *Freikorps* was in existence before WWI there, Sheriff."

Grandpa frowned. "What's the *Freikorps*?"

"It was a forerunner paramilitary culture founded to promote Aryan superiority…became the National Socialist German Workers…"

"Ooo, the Nazi Party."

Mister Tom nodded at grandpa.

I looked at Mister Tom. "What's an Aryan?"

He took a breath. "It's a group of white people in Germany who think they're racially superior to all other races...They believe they originated on the lost continent of Atlantis. They promoted that everyone in Eastern Europe must certify that their lineage be traced to Aryan descent back in the 30s."

The sheriff's mouth dropped open. "You're kiddin'?"

Mister Tom shook his head. "They believed they were the Master Race and that the Slavs, Gypsies, Jews, and Negroid races were racially inferior and should be eliminated...or enslaved."

Grandpa grimaced. "The start of WWII and the Holocaust."

I tugged on grandpa's pant leg. "What's the Ho-lo-caust, Grandpa?"

"The so-called Master Race, Foot, the Aryans, led by a man named Hitler, murdered some 11 million people before and during WWII, including over 6 million Jews and 5 million Gypsies, Slavs, Negroes, and some others..." He shook his head. "They're evil people."

Hutch took a breath. "Gol-uh-olee."

Mister Tom looked at him an' me. "Then the US got involved again."

THE POND

The sheriff turned back to Mister Tom. "You think that Eric Hoffer, or whatever his name is, may..."

Mister Tom shook his head again. "I think he's somehow important to the remaining underground Aryan movement still active in Germany...but he's not German...I believe he's a Jewish Gypsy on the run and...has something they want."

§§§

CHAPTER SIX

HAYNESVILLE ROAD

"Zey knew who he vas." Elias nodded and glanced over at Jonas at the wheel.

"*Ja*, zey did, but by different name." He thought for a moment. "Maybe ve check mit ze property records at ze court house in El Dorado."

"Did you notice ze skull on ze table?"

"*Ja*…Old."

Elias nodded again. "*Ja*...mit two bullet hole in forehead..."

"Execution style...like ze *freiheitskämpfers*, so-called freedom fighters, in ze Fatherland did."

"Ve vill find hem."

JAMISON HOME

The doc looked at Sheriff Wilson, then grandpa an' Mister Tom. "Going to take me a couple of days to completely examine those skeletons. See if there's any other signs of trauma, or if the gunshots were it."

The sheriff kinda cocked his head. "Don't you think the bullets to the head would be enough?"

The doc raised both his eyebrows. "What if they were tortured first?"

Mister Tom nodded. "Think I agree with the doc. Believe there almost had to be some prelude to the execution. Didn't have to get up close and personal to kill them."

Hutch leaned over to me. "What's pre-lude?"

I shook my head 'cause I got no idea at all what prelude means, either. But I'm guessin' Mister

Tom's talkin' 'bout some stuff goin' on 'fore they were killed—makes sense to me. Kinda like they do in some of those spy type pitchur shows—always somethin' happenin' leadin' up to killin's.

I looked up an' saw a new 1950 light green four door Ford with a sun visor over the windshield pull up out front. Daddy, mama, an' Bobby, my older brother by three years, got out an' headed up to the house.

Don't have a watch, but must be after three 'cause that's when daddy gets home—he was on the daylight tower this week. It's only 'bout five miles from our house in Junction City out here to grandpa's, so it don't take long to get here.

Daddy grinned as he an' mama climbed up the stoop—he always liked comin' to grandma an' grandpa's, like me. Bobby jumped up an' sat beside me, Tiny, an' Hutch on the edge of the porch.

"Well, looks like a meetin' of the minds…Why do I smell trouble?"

Mama shook her head as she opened the screen door. "Because there usually is when Sheriff Wilson and Doctor Duckworth are here at the same time."

THE POND

She didn't let the door slam behind her as she headed to the kitchen where grandma was to help with supper.

I leaned over to Hutch an' whispered, "Bet a nickel everbody's stayin' for supper."

He shook his head. "No bet."

Daddy looked over at the doc. "Do I need to ask why you're holdin' a skull, Doctor Duckworth?"

"Kind of a long story, Joe." He grinned an' glanced down at it, then around at everbody else. "Anybody want to fill him in?"

Grandma came out the screen door with three cookies an' three glasses of buttermilk on a tray for me, Bobby, an' Hutch. "All you get, boys, don't want to spoil your supper." She turned an' went back inside.

Grandpa leaned back in his rockin' chair. "Well, guess it's up to me..." He glanced over at me. "Unless you want to do it, Foot."

I just shook my head, I wanted to eat my cookie.

He looked back at daddy as he pulled another rocker up. "Foot and Hutch found this skull in

Dud's pond when they went swimmin' yesterday…"

'Bout twenty minutes later, grandpa was near finished. "…we brought both skeletons up here so Doc can take 'em in to do what he does. Then by some strange coincidence…"

"No such thing."

Grandpa nodded. "Probably right about that, Joe…anyway these two fellows with German accents came by right after we got back to the house. One of them was real interested in that skull there…and the bullet holes in it. It was just sittin' on that little table behind us…Said they were lookin' for a friend. A Motshan…." He glanced at Mister Tom.

"Bieler."

"Right, Motshan Beiler. We never heard the name before, but Tom says it's a Jewish Gypsy name…That it may be Dud's real name."

"Are the Jews still being persecuted over there?"

THE POND

Tom nodded. "Yeah, especially the Jewish Gypsy's, Joe...by the remaining underground Aryans."

"Why?"

"One, they still think they are an inferior race, or group of people, and should be wiped out...and two, it's rumored they started hiding a lot of their wealth...gold, jewelry, art, and so on, even before WWI."

Daddy shook his head. "And the Nazis still stole train loads of it."

"Correct...but it's believed that was only a fraction."

"My, my...Years of intrigue."

Hutch leaned into me again. "What's intrigue?"

I shook my head again.

Bobby turned to us. "Means secret stuff like with perfidy."

I turned to Hutch. "Perfidy means deceitful or treacherous. Saw that word in a Edgar Rice Burroughs book I was readin'...one of my favorites, *Tarzan of the Apes*...looked it up. It was in *A Princess of Mars*, too...Think he liked the word."

Bobby'd had three more years of school than me or Hutch, he knew stuff—sometimes. Usually didn't hesitate to let me know 'bout it, neither. Always tryin' to make a point he was smarter'n me.

But, I knew some stuff, too, 'cause I read a lot of books, like from Mister Burroughs an' he always uses some words I gotta look up in the dictionary.

Daddy looked at Mister Tom, then the sheriff. "Think they were up to no good, then?"

"Bet my life on it…Spent quite a bit of time in Germany after the war. Got to know a bunch of those Aryans…Very single-minded group of people. There's only one way…Their way."

The doc nodded. "Well, like I said, going to take me a day or so to completely analyze those skeletons." He glanced at the sheriff. "I suggest holding off doing anything till we have more information."

Sheriff Wilson kinda mashed his lips together. "For once I agree with you…Damned old quack."

"Well, for a lawman who got his badge out of a Cracker Jack box…you should."

"I'll have you know jaybird…"

THE POND

Mama stuck her head out the door. "Supper's ready. Figured everybody was staying so mama fixed plenty. But she always does anyway…Ya'll need to wash up."

Doc Duckworth got to his feet first. "I'll go add this with the rest of the skeleton. Sure glad I kept them in separate sacks." He walked out the path to the sheriff's car, opened the trunk, put the skull in what I figured was the sack that didn't have one, and came back to the porch.

"Wonder what grandma fixed for suppper? All I been smellin' is peach cobbler."

Daddy turned to me as he was openin' the screen door. "Think I heard your mother say something about cat's ass an' cabbage, Hoss Fly."

Hutch elbowed me in the ribs and frowned. "Is that for real?"

I grinned an' shook my head. "Uh-uh, daddy says that all the time…an' we've never had it yet. Hadn't seen no cats around, anyway. Think he's always kiddin'…Least I hope so."

Hutch shook his head. "Yeah, me too."

Me an' Hutch went down to the wash stand at the far end of the porch to wash our feet first, on account grandma said they were dirty an' not to come in her house with 'em that way. Dang sure wadn't gonna argue with her—that wadn't ever smart. Everbody else went down the dog run to the wash stand at the end by the kitchen.

We got all washed up an' took our places at grandma's long ol' table. Me, Hutch an' Bobby sat on the bench on the west side, while the grownups got the chairs on the other. Grandpa an' grandma sat in the chairs with arms on 'em at each end.

Tiny took her place under the table by my feet.

Mama an' grandma was makin' trips from the kitchen to the table carryin' two bowls or platters apiece each time.

Sheriff Wilson took a sip of his tea an' looked down at grandpa. "We just as well plan the fishin' trip for this weekend, John. Got anyplace in particular you think about going to?"

Grandpa set his mug of clabber back down on the table an' wiped the white mustache off with the back of his hand. "What about below Lock Seven on the Ouachita River. Hear there's some big channel cat there."

Daddy nodded. "Agree, Myron. That bluff above the bend is a prime place to fish the channel."

THE POND

"I've got a new batch of stink bait been itchin' to try."

"What's it made of, Tom?"

He looked at daddy.

I leaned over to Hutch. "Hope he don't say cat's ass an' cabbage."

"Ground up calf brains an' limburger cheese…been rottin' for nearly three weeks."

"Tom Rayford! Not at my table."

"Oh, sorry Miz Mame, didn't notice you'd come back in with that big platter of roast beef."

Grandpa an' daddy both kinda giggled. They knew how grandma was 'bout stuff like that. But, ain't nothin' nastier'n in the whole world than stink bait—but the catfish sure seem to like it.

"We can have JB drive his pickup. He's got one of those new tin ice chests to put the fish in," offered grandpa.

The sheriff reached for the roast beef with his fork, got a big chunk, then a spoonful of grandma's mashed potatoes an' poured a dollop of gravy over the top an' the roast beef.

"Good idea, John, I'll get some sponges in El Dorado to cut up when I get home an' meet ya'll in Lawson on the way."

Sponges are the best thing to use with stink bait. You cut 'em in chunks an' put 'em on your hooks—we usually rig up double hooks on our lines—wet it, then push it down in the stink bait with a stick.

Boy howdy, sure don't want to get any on your hands. Smell's enough to gag a maggot if you forget an' pick your nose.

Daddy had a big grin on his face. "Been thinking about a good old fashioned fish fry all summer. Nothin' better than channel cat fried in lard in a big cast iron wash pot over a good hot hickory fire.

Grandma put her hands on her hips—she didn't have none, but she put 'em there anyway. "Well, I would suggest you focus on that roast beef, mashed potatoes an' gravy, fried squash and okra before you think about eating a platter of fried fish, Joe Lee...or you won't get any of my peach cobbler."

Daddy looked up kinda sheepishly. "Yessum."

Doctor Duckworth groaned an' nodded. "That's about right, leave me here doing all the work while ya'll go fishing...Thanks a lot."

Sheriff Wilson shrugged. "Some days chicken, some days feathers, Ralph...I'm sure you'll be first in line with your plate when Mame goes to dippin' those catfish filets out of the pot."

"Got that right, you old goat."

Mister Tom looked up from his plate an' glanced at grandpa, the sheriff an' the doc. "Don't suppose ya'll noticed the bulges under the arms of those two fellows."

Grandpa, Sheriff Wilson, an' Doctor Duckworth exchanged glances. Daddy just cocked his eyebrow at the information 'cause he wadn't there.

"Were wearing shoulder holsters. Five'll get you ten both were carrying Lugers."

§§§

CHAPTER SEVEN

UNION COUNTY COURTHOUSE

"Vell, ze zign on ze door says closed until Monday. Ve forgot zese lazy Americans don't vork on ze veekends." Jonas pulled the handle on the locked door on the east side of the courthouse at 5:30 on Friday afternoon. "And ze are already closed for ze day."

"Vhat now?"

THE POND

The two men turned and walked back to their car.

"Ve vait..." Becker stopped abruptly before they reached their vehicle. "...Unless."

"Unless, vhat?"

"Maybe...maybe zhey vill go see Beiler to tell hem two men are looking for hem." He looked over at Webber. "Ve follow...*Ja*?"

"*Ja*."

JAMISON HOME

The sky was still dark, but there was this light rosy glow along to the east right at the tops of the trees. We finished breakfast an' grandma an' mama had fixed a big basket of sandwiches an' stuff for lunch, 'long with a gallon jug of tea.

Mister Tom had walked the short mile from his house over by Jolley's Chapel Cemetery with three pint Mason jars of his stink bait. He had 'em all padded up with towels—dang sure didn't want to bust one of 'em. Daddy fixed a place in the trunk for 'em 'long with everbody's fishin' gear.

The rod an' reels were on the top of the car in a special rack daddy had built out at the rig just for fishin' trips.

We managed to find places to sit in daddy's car. Bobby got in the front with daddy an' grandpa an' Mister Tom was in the back with me an' Hutch. Unka JB would be drivin' his pickup an' takin' Don an' Hubert with 'im. They just pulled up at the side of the house next to daddy's Ford.

Daddy cut through the back roads to Lawson—grandpa knew all the country roads in the area. We met Sheriff Wilson there an' scrunched up in the back seat for Bobby on 'count the sheriff wanted to ride up front with grandpa after puttin' his gear in the trunk with ours.

It was only 'bout fifteen or so miles from Lawson to Lock 7 an' that bend we was gonna fish at on the Ouachita. Sun was just above the trees when we pulled up at that big bluff.

It was 'round fifteen feet above the river that made a fair hard horseshoe bend an' the channel was right at the bottom of the bluff—that's where all the channel an' blue cat would be. They liked the faster movin' water more'n the yellow an' flatheads—why they were better eatin', grandpa told me.

We got all unloaded an' everbody picked spots along the bluff to cast out into the river from. Me, Hutch, Bobby, Don, an' Hubert had one rod an' reel each while daddy, grandpa, Unka JB, the sheriff, an' Mister Tom each had two.

Everbody rigged their lines up with two hooks spaced 'bout foot an' a half apart above the lead sinker that was at the end of the line. Each hook had a chunk of sponge threaded on it that we soaked in Mister Tom's stink bait.

Made sure we were plenty far apart when we cast out into the channel, didn't want to sling'ny off on anybody—'specially one of the grownups.

We had all cut us a forked stick to shove in the ground to prop the rods on while the grownups sat back under a shade tree what was close an' waited for that reel to sing.

It wadn't over thirty minutes from when we drove up that everbody had lines in the water. It was fishin' time.

I like to sit behind my rod with the line comin' out of my reel over my finger. I could feel when a big ol' cat would go to suckin' on that sponge.

They'd suck on it a bit, then take it in their mouth an' swim off. That's when I'd pick up my rig, give it a big jerk with the tip, settin' that hook—then the fight was on.

Fightin' a big ol' fish, or sometimes two on the double rig, up to the top of the water an' over to the bank is got to be just about the most fun a feller can have at one time.

Your rod will bend dang near double sometimes an' whip back an' forth as that cat would try to get away while you worked him up from the bottom.

Grandpa said it was probably better'n fifty feet deep from the top to the bottom of the channel—lot's of room for 'em to fight. Had to get 'em up some so they didn't run under an' old sunk limb or somethin'. Heck you could lose your whole hook an' sinker riggin' an' have to completely rebuild it. That's why I like to keep my finger on the line.

THE POND

I looked over at Hutch, he was 'bout twenty feet away with his spot. "Hutch, think I got one playin' with one of my hooks."

"Watch 'im."

"Am."

My line went tight an' my reel started singin'. I picked my rod up—popped the tip back almost over my head.

"Hot dang... Got 'im!"

I jumped to my feet.

"Keep your tip up!"

"What do you think I'm doin'?"

"Let him run a little."

"Gotta get him off the bottom first, ding-a-ling."

I cranked a dozen turns on my reel, then set the brake to let him fight an' tire his self out. Figured he was 'bout ten feet off the bottom.

Fifty yards back up toward the dirt road, two blond-headed blue-eyed men in khakis watched Foot fight the fish on his line through a set of binoculars.

"Is zat all zhey are doing, Jonas, yust fishing zat river?"

"Apparently zo."

He looked up from the eyepieces. "Haven't zeen anyone vhat could be Beiler, yet."

"Do ve continue?"

"*Ja*...Zey vill eventually contact hem. I am positive."

"Do ve stay?"

"*Nein*, ve go and vatch the house for vhen zey come home...Ve must be patient, *freund*."

"*Ja*, zhere is a great deal at stake."

Had that sucker at the bottom of the bluff on top of the water an' slowly reeled him up the side. I backed up an' pulled him over the edge.

"Hotamighty dang, look at that. Must weigh four or five pounds. Gotta be near two feet long...Woowee!"

I stuck my fingers under his gills an' pulled the pliers I had brought from my back pocket an' worked the hook from his lip. Sure glad he didn't swallow it. That's what happens when you don't set the hook quick.

THE POND

"Be right back, gonna go put this bad boy in Unka JB's cooler."

"Ain't goin' no…Holy cow, got a runner."

Hutch picked up his rod an' set the hook like I did. Looked like he had a fight on his hands, too.

"Don't lose 'im."

"Ain't." He lifted the tip of his rod high an' played 'im like I did.

I walked upriver toward where Unka JB an' them were fishin' an' found the cooler. There were already three nice cats in it almost the same size as mine. Yessir, gonna be a good day.

I looked up to see both daddy an' Mister Tom walkin' my way. Daddy had one by the lip in each hand an' Mister Tom just had one, but it was a real dandy. They were doin' good, too.

"Wow, those look fine, Daddy."

"You get one, too, Hoss Fly?"

I held mine up from the cooler.

He grinned. "I'd say."

"That's a nice one, Foot."

"Yours too, Mister Tom…Gonna have a Jim Cracker fish fry this evenin'."

He nodded. "Yep, doesn't get much better'n this."

Daddy put his in the cooler 'long with Mister Tom's. "Keeps up and this cooler'll be full by noon."

We turned around an' saw Hutch comin' up with his catch. He couldn't hold it all the way off the ground—the tail was draggin'. Thought his face was gonna break if he grinned any bigger.

"Hutch, that feller weighs seven pounds if he weighs an ounce." Daddy looked impressed.

He looked at Mister Tom. "I'd say your stink bait has been a real success, Tom...Maybe you ought to make up a large batch and sell it. Might go big."

A grin spread across his face, too. It's amazin' what a good day fishin' will do for folks. Can't really be described, reckon someone would just have to experience it—bringin' home a real mess of fish is better'n Christmas mornin'.

Sure 'nuff, by high noon Unka JB's cooler was chock plumb full. Took both him an' daddy to pick it up.

THE POND

Grandpa shook his head. "Hate to quit when we're on a run, but we got more'n we can eat...Waste not, want not."

I looked over at him. "Who said that, Grandpa? Seems I've heard it before."

He grinned. Looked like everbody was grinnin' today.

"Now whose lips were moving when you heard it, Foot?"

I ducked my head. "Uh...Oh, you did. That's where I heard it before."

He nodded. "Uh-huh..." Grandpa looked at everbody that had gathered 'round. "Well, let's load up, people, got a mess of fish to clean an' skin when we get home...Mame, Vertis, an' Thelma will want 'em ready to filet an' cut up for mealin'."

Grandpa divied up the sandwiches, then we got everthin' loaded back in the vehicles an' headed back toward the house.

Two men in a black Ford were parked a quarter mile to the south from Smead Jolley's store. The one named Elias watched through the binoculars as a light green Ford sedan, the sheriff's Buick, and then a dark blue 1948 GMC pickup pull off the Haynesville Road onto the dirt road that led down to Big John Jamison's house.

"Ze are back."

§§§

CHAPTER EIGHT

JAMISON HOME

We pulled up under the shade of the sycamore trees, parked, an' all bailed out. Daddy an' Unka JB grabbed the heavy cooler an' toted it to the side of the house where the table was for cleanin' fish, squirrels or whatever game there was to clean.

Tiny was runnin' in big circles about the yard, up on the porch, back down, an' around our legs. She didn't get to go on account there wasn't enough room in daddy's car with all of us an' she was happy we were back. She'd tire out in a bit an' then stick to me like glue.

I tapped the sheriff on the elbow. "Uh…Sheriff Wilson."

He turned an' looked down at me. "What is it, Foot?"

"Did you notice that black Ford parked down the way back on the Haynesville Road?"

He glanced at Mister Tom who was standin' close by at the cleanin' table 'long with grandpa, daddy, an' Unka JB, where they were all gonna work deheadin', guttin', an' peelin' the skin off'n those big catfish, then back at me.

"What about it?"

"Purty sure it's the same car those two fellas that talked funny that were here yesterday were drivin'."

"You sure?"

"I seen it too, Sheriff," Hutch popped up.

Mister Tom nodded. "Wouldn't surprise me at all, Sheriff, if they're who I think they are."

Everbody looked at Mister Tom.

He kinda grimaced a bit. "The *Freikorps*…reinvigorated Aryan underground."

THE POND

Grandpa cleared his throat. "You think they're watching to see if we contact Eric Hoffer or whatever his name is."

He nodded. "The one they call Motshan Bieler...They think we'll lead them to him."

The sheriff removed his hat an' rubbed his baldin' head. "Well, we are going to have to talk with him tomorrow...especially after Ralph finishes his analysis of those bones...no question about that."

He looked down at me again. "Good job, Foot...You too, Hutch. Way to go keepin' your eyes open...We could all learn a thing or too from these boys."

The sheriff patted me an' Hutch both on the head. We both grinned 'cause I guess we did good.

He turned to grandpa. "Any idea how we can go talk with Dud or Eric, John?"

"Only one way that they can't follow us."

"And that would be?"

"Through my property back down to the pond and on past it to his cabin. I know where it is...A bit of a walk, but pretty darn secluded."

"I suspect they'll try to keep a watch on anyone leaving John's by car. Won't be able to see us go in the gate and across the pasture to the woods from the road…They'll never know we left the house to go down there."

The sheriff nodded. "Good thinkin', Tom…You're right. If they somehow happen to see us go that way and try to follow…Well, I do believe that would be trespassin'…Wouldn't you say, John?"

"I would…Don't take kindly to trespassers."

"Can we go?"

Grandpa glanced at daddy an' I saw him shake his head. "No, you boys stay here…Will look better if they see ya'll playin' in the yard. You can be a big help that way."

Me an' Hutch both nodded. Knew we were bein' stroked but figured it would be best not to say nothin'.

Mama came out the back door with a pan to put the first cuts an' filets in so she, grandma, aunt Thelma, an' my cousin, Jessie could start rollin' 'em in cornmeal, salt an' pepper.

They had already been peelin' taters to slice up for fryin'—saw Jessie throw the peelin's out in the yard for the chickens.

THE POND

Hutch's grandparents, Mamie an' Raymond Grant walked in the yard from down Red Hill Road where they lived.

Mamie's job was to get a fire built under the big iron wash pot—a different one than she boiled our clothes in—an' a smaller one next to it so they could fill 'em half full of lard for the fish an' taters.

Hutch's grandpa, Raymond, was to do the cookin'. He was 'bout the best fish fry man in the county—grandma said.

Grandma an' them also was makin' up a big bowl of coleslaw. Grandpa had a good cabbage crop this year. There was gonna be plenty for everbody.

Mama an' Jessie had gone berry pickin' while we were fishin' this mornin'. Grandma was fixin' a ginormous pan of dewberry cobbler for desert.

In 'bout an hour, we had that big cooler of catfish gutted, deheaded, skint, an' cut up for grandma an them.

Me an' Hutch had carried the guts, heads, skin, an' bones out to the hogs. They'd make short work of 'em.

Hutch's grandpa announced that the grease was ready in both pots so mama an' aunt Thelma started bringin' out pans of mealed catfish an' sliced up taters for 'im.

Grandpa, daddy, an' Unka JB had set up a couple of long plank tables out front in the shade of the sycamores.

Grandma an' them had put the coleslaw an' cobbler on one of the tables an' covered it with a big white sheet thing to keep the flies off. There was also a couple bottles of Del Monte Ketchup sittin' on the table—I like ketchup with my fish but they don't need much of anythin' else. Boy-hidy, won't be long now.

Hutch's grandpa looked over at grandma as she stepped out the back door with a empty pan. "Right on time, Mame, fish an' the taters are ready, you can start dippin' 'em out."

Mama came out behind her with another pan for the French fries.

We all grabbed a plate an' lined up at the empty table where mama an' them would be settin' the steamin' hot fish an' taters as grandma dipped 'em out of the boilin' grease. 'Course grandpa, daddy an' them went first—that was just the way it was.

THE POND

Everbody started loadin' their plates up. I had a stack of fish, a pile of taters, an' a small dab of coleslaw with a dollop of ketchup between the fish an' taters. I grabbed a Mason jar of sweet iced tea from the table an' moved to the porch to sit down on the edge with my plate in my lap. Dang, it smelled good.

Hutch sat down beside me an' Tiny was in her usual place between us waitin' for her tidbits.

Bobby, Don, an' Hubert also found places on the edge of the porch to sit with their plates—there was plenty of room.

Grandpa an' the other men sat down in the chairs, 'cept Mister Tom an' he picked a spot on the stoop.

Grandma, mama, aunt Thelma, an' Jessie would eat last on account they were still ferryin' the fish an' taters from the pots to the tables. That's what women did.

Grandpa set his plate on the little table up on the porch an' cleared his throat. "Everybody, listen up, before ya'll get too involved with your food, we need to say Grace."

Everbody looked up, stopped eatin', an' bowed their heads.

85

"Gracious Heavenly Father, we give humble thanks for this wonderful bounty you have provided today. We also thank you for the fellowship of family and friends. May you continue to guide an' protect each and everyone here today. Bless this food to the nourishment of our bodies and our bodies to thy Holy service. These things we ask in Jesus' Holy Name…Amen."

Everbody added a 'Amen', an' then went back to eatin'.

"Zo vhat are zey doing now?" Elias Webber shook a cigarette from the pack of Eckstein No. 5 German cigarettes he took from his shirt pocket.

"Praying." Jonas Becker took the field glasses down from his eyes and glanced at his partner.

Elias' head jerked up from lighting his cigarette with his IMCO German lighter. "Praying?"

"*Ja*. Zayin' prayer before zey eat."

He lit his smoke and blew a cloud out the open window beside him. "Ah."

"Zee anyone new?"

"*Nein*…Yust two older Negros…Zey vere servants doin' ze cooking."

THE POND

"Zhey get fish and potatoes vile ve get zese stale bologna zandviches from ze ztore down ze road."

Elias took a wax paper wrapped sandwich from a brown bag on the seat between them. "And it is not even good bologna like back home."

"Ve vill finish our job zoon...an' zen ve can go back." Jonas dug his own sandwich from the bag.

Grandpa glanced over at Mister Tom. "They still watchin'?"

Mister Tom didn't look up from his plate. He just nodded.

"Yeah, they moved a little closer an' are watching us through field glasses. Saw a glint through their windshield a bit ago."

The sheriff smiled after swallowing a bite of filet he'd bit off. "Thought as much...They're about as close as they can get and from that angle, won't be able to see us go through the gate by the barn tomorrow."

Grandma looked up from her plate over by the food tables where she, mama, aunt Thelma, an'

Jessie were standin' eatin'. "Ya'll be sure to save room for the cobbler."

Mister Tom glanced over from his place on the stoop an' chuckled. "Don't think there's any worry about that, Mame...always make room for your cobbler...always."

We looked up as a new gray Pontiac pulled up out front an' Doctor Duckworth got out.

"Well, look who just happened to drop by."

The doc opened the gate an' headed toward the tables. "No thanks to you, you old goat. I hope you choke...Anything left, Mame?"

"Of course, Ralph. I was fixing to carry some inside to put in the warming oven for you. Figured you'd show up sometime."

He glared at the sheriff. "Some of us have work to do."

Grandma handed him a loaded plate of fish, fries, an' slaw. "Appreciate it, Mame, looks scrumptious."

Now I don't know what 'scrumptious' means, but I'm gonna take a guess it has somethin' to do with purty good.

"Well, what'd you find out, you old quack?"

THE POND

The doc picked up a big catfish filet an' crunched off a bite. "Umm good, Mame…outstanding."

He chewed real slowly, not that the fish needed it 'cause it would melt in your mouth. Figured he was doin' it on purpose just to irritate his best friend, the sheriff—they grew up together, grandpa said.

He nodded. "Worth the wait."

The doc finally looked up an' over to the sheriff who looked like he was turnin' a bit red.

"I was right."

The sheriff rolled his eyes. "About what?"

"That they might have been tortured."

"And?"

He took another bite, chewed it even slower, an' never looked back up as he grabbed a long French fry an' swiped it through some ketchup.

"They were."

§§§

CHAPTER NINE

JAMISON HOME

The sheriff an' Doc Duckworth showed back up just as we got home from church. Grandma didn't fix any Sunday dinner like she normally did on account there was fish left an' she knew it wouldn't keep in her ice box.

Her an' mama made some tater salad before we left for the services 'cause cold French fries aren't near as good as cold fried chicken or fish. But her tater salad is somethin' special.

She also made a couple of apple pies with fresh apples from Mister Tom's orchard I was hankerin' to dig into. Could smell the cinnamon-apple aroma when we came in the house.

We had already changed clothes an' Hutch came up after the colored services at their church were over, too.

He leaned over to me at the table. "What're we gonna do since we can't go over to Unka Dud's with the grownups?"

I dumped a big spoonful of tater salad on my plate next to the fish. Grandma also fried up a batch of hot water cornbread in bacon grease—some folks call 'em cornpones, hush puppies, or corn dodgers, but I've always just called 'em what they are—hot water cornbread. You can tote 'em around in your pocket for later, too. Grandma makes patties 'bout the size of her hand.

Daddy looked across the table. "What are you boys going to be up to while we're gone?"

I shrugged my shoulders. "Oh, we'll get into somethin', I 'magine."

THE POND

"I'm sure you will." He nodded an' looked over at Bobby an' them. "What about ya'll? Going to do something with Foot an' Hutch?"

They looked at each other, then Bobby turned back to daddy.

"Uh-uh, they're just kids. We're goin' squirrel huntin' down on the other side of Yankee meadow. Gonna take some bacon an' fish for crawdads in that branch down there on the way back."

Bobby was always sayin' stuff like that...Even though Hubert wadn't no older'n me, him an' Don got along good, lot's better'n us.

Bobby thinks bein' three years older'n me makes him a grownup or somethin'. Daddy just looked at him an' kinda arched one eyebrow.

"Uh-huh."

"If ya'll're goin' squirrel hunting, bring home enough and I'll make squirrel an' dumplings for supper."

Him, Don, an' Hubert all nodded at grandma. "Yessum."

"Anybody zhow up besides ze zheriff's car?" Elias pitched a cigarette butt out his window.

Jonas shook his head as he lowered the field glasses. "*Nein*. Yust it…Ze doctor vas mit him."

"Zink zey came to yust eat Zunday dinner?"

"*Ja*…zat an' maybe plan to go zee Beiler, maybe." Jonas looked over at Elias.

"Ve can't zee ze front of ze house from zis angle…Maybe ve zould drive over for ze visit?"

Jonas put the glasses back up to his eyes. "Maybe, in bit…Two of ze boys have come to ze zide of ze house mit a blanket…an' ze older boys left an' are valkin' down ze other road down hill mit rifles."

"Ze go hunting?"

"*Ja*."

"Here, spread this old quilt that grandma's lettin' us use." I flipped it open an' we laid it out on the ground.

"What'd you got in mind?"

I pulled two comic books from where I had 'em rolled up in the back pocket of my bib overalls.

"What're those?"

"These are the first two issues of a new comic book that's out…*Judo Joe*."

THE POND

"*Judo Joe?*"

"Yeah, he's a guy that uses this fightin' style, think it's from Japan or somewhere like that, to fight the bad guys…It's called Judo."

We sat down on the quilt an' I opened the first one an' started showin' it to Hutch.

"Gol-uh-olee! Look at that."

"Yeah, an' see, looky here…Each episode shows how to do one of those Judo throws…step-by-step. Let's see if we can learn how to do 'em…What say?"

His eyes got big. "Yeah!"

We went to the back an' I pointed out the important stuff—I had already read it a bunch of times.

He looked down at the page. "Says it don't matter how big somebody is, that you can use their own weight an' mo-men-tum against 'em…" He glanced up at me. "What's mo-mem-tum?"

"Well, the dictionary had a bunch of gobbledygook, but basically means once somethin' gets goin' in one direction, it's hard to stop."

"Huh?"

"If some bully goes to chargin' at you, well, you just help him on past by usin' his own speed an' weight...His momentum."

"Uh...right."

"Here, get up an' I'll show you." I laid the comics off to the side an' I got in the middle of the quilt. "Now, run at me like you're gonna knock me on my butt."

"Really?"

"Yep, just do it."

"Ok, you asked for it."

He put his head down an' charged at me. I stepped a little to the side, grabbed his overalls an' slung him past me stumblin' off balance, completely off the quilt to the dirt.

He sat up an' spit some of the sand he'd picked up out of his mouth, blinked his eyes a couple times an' looked back at me still standin' in the center of the quilt.

"Wow!...Never saw that comin'."

"That's the point. That's momentum...Yours."

"Let's see some more of that stuff." He got up an' stepped back on the quilt.

"The throw in this issue is called the *Hip Toss*."

"*Hip Toss*?"

THE POND

"Uh-huh. Looky here." I laid the book down again. "Now, say you reach out to grab me or shove me in the chest…Go ahead."

Hutch reached out both hands to push me like a bully might do. I stepped one foot forward an' cross his two feet, wrapped my left arm around his waist, grabbed his left arm with my right, twisted an' put my hip in his middle, bent over a little an' yanked with my arm that was around him an' by the arm I had hold of, pullin' him off balance. He flipped over my hip an' landed flat on his back with a massive *whoosh* as most of his air came out.

"Ahhhh." He rolled over tryin' to get his breath.

"You awright?"

He blinked his big brown eyes a couple of times as he laid on his back trying to suck air in. Hutch finally got a couple of breaths, looked up at me, nodded an' mouthed a *wow*—no sound came out, though.

"Oh, meant to tell you to blow all your air out before you grabbed me."

He took a breath an' got to his feet. "Now you tell me."

THE POND

"See how I used your momentum? Now you try it."

"Uh-huh." He took a couple more deep breaths, then stood in the middle where I had been.

"Do it real slow, like 1-2-3-4…"

"Right."

I reached out to grab his shoulders. Hutch did the steps like doin' a dance or somethin'. He stepped forward, grabbed my arm, put his hip in my waist, pulled an' bent over an' I went flyin'—landed on my back as I let my air out on the way.

"Wow!" He looked down at my grinnin' face.

"See?"

"Holy cow!…Let's do it some more."

We practiced the hip toss till we could do it real quick without havin' to think about the steps. Daddy always told me that a person never does anything well until they quit thinkin' 'bout how to do it. Gotta say he's right—'course he most always is.

THE POND

I picked up the second issue of *Judo Joe* an' flipped to the back. "The next one is the *Shoulder Throw*."

"Boy hidy, I'm afraid to ask."

We studied the diagrams together.

Hutch pointed at the pitchurs. "You know, looks to me like it could be a little easier if the person you're throwin' is taller'n you."

I looked at them, cocked my head a little an' turned to him. "I say, Ollie, I think you've got it."

Hutch frowned. "Who's Ollie?"

"A comedy team from the movies, Laurel an' Hardy. One of the guys is a Englishman named Stan Laurel an' he was always referrin' to the other fella, Oliver Hardy, as 'Ollie'."

He shook his head. "You must see a lots of movies."

"When mama an' daddy let me durin' the winter. Nothin' else 'sides readin' books an' listenin' to the radio…'Course I like readin' books most as good as watchin' movies…maybe better."

We started practicin' the *Shoulder Throw* just like we had the *Hip Toss* an' after a hour or so, got purty good at that, too.

THE POND

Me an' Hutch folded up the quilt after shakin' the sand an' grass off so we could go inside an' get a drink of water. Would have to wait till next month for the next issue to learn another throw.

I looked at him as we went in the back door. "You know, we oughta start a Judo club an' learn a new move ever month."

"Okay, sounds neat. What are we gonna call it?"

Uh…How about the F & H Judo Club?"

He frowned. "What's wrong with the H & F Judo Club?"

I finished the dipper of water an handed it to Hutch. "Well, on account of I thought of it…How do you like them apples?"

He got his drink an' we headed down the dog run to the front door. "Well, guess you got a point…but next time I get to name it."

"Okay…Wanna play marbles?"

"Sure…Our marbles are in that drawer in that little table on the porch. I'll get 'em."

He took the two bags out of the drawer an' we stepped down the stoop to the yard. I drew a circle in the sand with my big toe.

THE POND

Hutch handed me my sack an' we knelt down at the edge of the ring just as that black Ford drove up out front. The two men that talked funny got out…

§§§

CHAPTER TEN

JAMISON HOME

The two men looked at the sheriff's car an'
daddy's, then opened the gate to the yard.

The hair on Tiny's back stood up an' she was
growlin' deep in her throat. Me an' Hutch got to
our feet.

They walked up to us an' looked down at me.

"Your grandfather here, son?"

I looked the one talkin' in the eye. "Not your son."

He nodded. "Iz ze sheriff or your grandfather here?"

I pointed out at the sheriff's Buick. "There's the sheriff's car…Who wants to know?"

The men glanced at each other, then the one that had been talkin' looked back down at me.

"You zeem to lack respect, young man."

"I respect folks that earn it, mister. My dog don't like you or your friend an' that's good enough for me…she's a pretty good judge of people."

He kinda gritted his teeth. "Vhere iz ze sheriff or doctor?"

"What makes you think the doctor's here?"

They looked puzzled—think they knew they'd been caught.

The other man turned to the first one. "Zhey know vhere zhey are. I zink ve should make zem tell us…I vill start mit ze *Neger* here."

He reached down for Hutch's shoulder—mistake.

Hutch crossed his foot in front of the man, pivoted his hips an' put his left hand up an' under the man's right arm. He grabbed the front of his coat, pulling him off balance an' threw him over his shoulder to the ground—did all that 'fore I could even blink. The man landed with a thud an' a *whoosh* as all his air left him.

"Elias!"

That fella stepped forward. I automatically moved to the position of a hip toss an' flipped him over my hip to his back where he lost his air, too.

Tiny jumped on one of his legs an' started chewin' an' shakin' his pant leg—growlin' an' snarlin' all the while. She tore a good chunk of the material away.

Both fellas moaned an' gasped for their breath. The first one started breathin' better—reached under his coat an' pulled his Luger gun out.

The whole yard seemed to vibrate with an explosion that hurt my ears. Leaves an' twigs from the sycamore branches overhead started fallin' like rain.

"Boys, step back from those men...get Tiny away, too. Come over toward me."

I looked up to see grandma standin' at the stoop with grandpa's long double barreled shotgun at her shoulder—looked almost big as her.

Me an' Hutch moved away from 'em an' toward the porch, like she said.

"Got another load of double ought buckshot here…Which one of you wants it?"

They glanced at each other—they were still layin' on their backs.

"What I thought…Now, get shed of those guns and pitch 'em to the side…Do it now! You don't want me to repeat myself." She waved the barrel of that shotgun from one to the other.

They chunked their Lugers over in grandma's flower beds.

"Now get to your feet."

They got up, a little shaky, both put their hands on their knees an' took a couple of breaths.

"Now, you have five seconds to get in that car and get off of our property…Two…three…"

They glanced at each other again an' one of 'em started to open his mouth but I guess he thought better of it. Both of 'em turned an' ran as fast as they were able—looked like their backs was hurtin' 'em some.

"…four…five."

THE POND

When grandma hit five, their car was already turning on the dirt road that went to down the Haynesville Road.

Mama stepped out of the screen door behind grandma. The both of 'em had grins spread completely 'cross their faces.

Grandma turned an' leaned the shotgun against the wall next to the door, an' then came down the steps to where me an' Hutch were. Mama was already there huggin' us.

Grandma shook her head. "I never saw the like. Where'd ya'll learn those moves you pulled on those two?"

Me an' Hutch looked at each other—we were both grinnin', too. I pulled the *Judo Joe* comic books from my back pocket an' unrolled 'em.

"We started a Judo club this mornin'...Been practicin' some stuff they show in here." I held 'em up so her an' mama could see the covers.

"My word!...A comic book. Of all things."

We all turned when we heard the chain rattlin' through the gate down at the barn an' saw grandpa, daddy, Mister Tom, the sheriff, an' Doc Duckworth comin' fast as they could. Grandpa, the sheriff, an' the doc was holdin' 'em up some. Everbody had their guns in their hands, 'cept the doc an' that was just 'cause he didn't carry one.

Grandpa jerked the gate to the yard open. "What the hell's goin' on here?...Mame, I heard my shotgun."

She still had a grin 'cross her face. "Ya'll may have trouble believing it. Best you come up here and have a seat. We'll fill you in."

Mama turned toward Red Hill Road. "Here come Bobby, Don, an' Hubert on the run. I guess they heard the shotgun, too. Looks like they had a good hunt, though."

Hubert was always the one that had to tote the squirrels when they went huntin'. He had a purty good bunch hangin' over his shoulder—their feet were all tied together with a string.

Bobby was the first in the yard—he was carryin' daddy's Stevens seventeen shot .22 bolt action. "What's happenin'? Heard gun fire."

It was 'bout the same thing grandpa had said.

Grandma pointed at the stoop. "Ya'll sit down we were fixin' to tell what just happened.

Hubert laid that big mess of squirrels on the bottom step, Tiny was Johnny-on-the-spot to come over an' smell. He had to shoo her away.

THE POND

Fifteen minutes later, me, Hutch, an' grandma told everbody what had happened. I didn't know she an' mama had come to the door when they heard the two men drive up an' were standin' just inside—they saw an' heard everthing. Didn't come out with grandpa's shotgun till that one fella pulled his gun.

The sheriff got up, stepped down to the yard an' got those Lugers out of grandma's flower bed.

I looked at Hutch while the sheriff was doin' that. "Looks like you were right, Hutch."

He frowned. "'Bout what?"

"'Bout that shoulder throw workin' better when your opponent is taller'n you."

He grinned. "Oh, yeah, that…Uh-huh. Did work, didn't it? He hit the ground like a load of bricks."

"Bigger they are…harder they fall." Daddy turned to Bobby an' smiled. "So they're just kids, huh, bud?"

He just kinda shrugged but didn't say nothin', but I could tell the way he looked at me that he was a bit jealous.

"Can me an' Hubert join the Judo club?"

"Sure Don, we'll have another practice tomorrow an' go through the hip toss an' shoulder throw again for ya'll…Better be ready, though."

Me an' Hutch looked at each other an' grinned. Noticed Bobby didn't want to join.

Grandma glanced at grandpa. "Now, what about ya'll's trip over to see Dud.

He looked at the others. "Well, that's the thing, Mame. It was a good trek past the pond. Saw lots of squirrels busy gathering pecans, black walnuts, an' hickory nuts all the way and around his cabin…but he wasn't there."

Grandma frowned. "Not there?"

Grandpa shook his head. "Nope…Still a whisp of smoke comin' from the chimney, but no one was inside. Door wasn't locked, so we went in. Stove was still warm an' there was a half cup of coffee on the table…it was warm, too."

"Think he might have been out hunting?"

"Could have been, Vertis. His gun rack was empty. We called for him…nothing. Just vanished."

"He's got a vehicle, doesn't he?"

THE POND

Grandpa turned to grandma an' nodded. "Does…An old Dodge. It was there, but no Dud."

"Couldn't find any fresh tracks, either. Of course be pretty hard to see on the forest floor," added Mister Tom.

The sheriff took off his hat an' wiped the inside band with his hanky an' put it back on his head. "I'm more concerned with those two Germans that just left findin' him than I am us. I just want to talk to him about the bodies in his pond."

Grandma looked at him. "Do you think he put them there or that they could have been there when he bought the property?"

"Yes to both, Mame. That's why I want to talk with him."

"What do you think, Ralph?"

He shook his head at grandma. "No way of knowing. I'm just sure the bones are over thirty years old…could be quite a bit older…or not."

Grandma got to her feet. "Anyone for coffee?"

The sheriff grinned. "Thought you'd never ask, Mame. Could use a pick me up after that hike through the woods."

"I'll bring a tray. Vertis, you want to help me?"

"Of course, Mama."

They both went through the screen door an' headed to the kitchen at the other end of the house.

Grandpa looked at Don. "You boys best take those squirrels around to the side an' get 'em cleaned for your grandma. Wouldn't waste any time about it either...She's probably already got some dumplin dough made up and ready to go."

Don jumped up from where he was sittin' on the stoop. "Oh, gosh, near forgot, listenin' to all the goin's on." He looked at Hubert an' Bobby. "Ya'll come on, we can get 'er done in a shake."

Hubert slung the bunch of squirrels—they were a mix of fox an' grays—back over his shoulder an' him an' Bobby followed Don 'round the side of the house to the cleanin' table.

Mister Tom watched 'em leave. He got up an' grabbed one of the porch posts an' stared at the leaves an' twigs grandma had blown out of the tree overhead.

"Well, I think there's a whole lot more to all this than meets the eye." He turned around an' looked at the rest of us. "But, I suppose it's all going to come out...sooner or later."

§§§

CHAPTER ELEVEN

HAYNESVILLE ROAD

"Vhat yust happened?" Elias rubbed the back of his neck and glanced over at Jonas behind the wheel.

"Zink ve vere vaylaid by two children…embarrassing." He twisted in his seat trying to loosen up his back.

"Vhat did zhey use on us?"

"Zome kind of Oriental fighting ztyle. I have zeen it zomevhere before."

"Vhat about our guns?"

"Ve get new ones."

"Vhere?"

Jonas glared at his partner. "Zis is America. Von can buy guns almost anyvhere. Zey even have stores zhat only zell guns."

"Zhey do?"

"*Ja.*"

"Zink ve can get Lugers?...Zhey are better zhan ze American guns."

"*Ja*...Zhey have many zhey captured or confiscated vhen ze Fatherland fell."

Elias grimaced and nodded. "Vhat do ve do after we get new guns?"

"Ve keep looking for Beiler. Ve go to county records office in ze morning after ve get guns."

"*Ja*...Zink I need long hot bath at ze motel."

"*Ja.*"

JAMISON HOME

Mister Tom wiped his mouth with his napkin, leaned back in his chair an' grinned. "Well, Mame, as usual, your squirrel an' dumplins were excellent, thank you." He glanced across the table at Don, Hubert, an' Bobby. "Good job on the hunt, boys." Then he looked back at grandma. "And I thought I'd died an' gone to Heaven when I took that first bite of your buttermilk pie...Ummm-umm."

Grandma kinda blushed an' flicked her napkin at Mister Tom. "Oh, pshaw. Go on with you, Thomas Rayford."

"Gotta agree with Mister Tom, Grandma...your buttermilk pie is outta sight."

She wrinkled her forehead some—don't think she'd heard that term before. "Thank you, Foot...I think."

He glanced over at Sheriff Wilson. "So, what's your next move, Sheriff?"

"Still really need to contact Dud. Guess we just keep tryin'." He looked at grandpa. "Think the Germans can find that road to his log cabin?"

"Only by happenstance, Myron. It's not on the map anywhere...old loggin' road that cuts through my property. Easement to the loggers expired years ago...Only way to get to his place is through mine...and that's not goin' to happen."

Daddy took a sip of his after dinner coffee mama had brought him. "Wish I could help, but I have to be back out at the rig in the mornin'."

"Think we'll be in pretty good shape, Joe." The sheriff looked over at me an' Hutch an' smiled. "We'll sic the boys on 'em."

"What time do you get home from the rig, Joe?"

"Oh, close as we are here, usually around 3:00 in the afternoon or so, John, why?"

"Gonna do some harvestin' of the last planting of watermelons tomorrow...Maybe do a cuttin' an' tastin' after supper." Grandpa looked around the table. "How's that sound?"

"Me an' the doc invited?"

Grandpa glanced at Sheriff Wilson. "Don't know why not, Myron. Gonna have four different types to taste."

I kinda raised my eyebrows. "What kinds of melons did you plant this year, Grandpa?"

"Well, you know, my special Black Diamonds, Charleston Grays, an' this year added Crimson Sweets...Supposed to be the sweetest there is. 'Course will also have my special striped yella meat I've created over the years.

THE POND

Me an' Hutch exchanged grins, lookin' forward to tomorrow. "Can we help pick, Grandpa?"

"Why sure, Foot. Was countin' on all you boys helpin'."

"What time you startin', John? I'll come help too."

"Right after breakfast, Tom. Get 'em picked an' in the shade before it gets hot tomorrow...Always appreciate the help."

We had the cuttin' an' tastin' under the trees on the long tables at the side of the house where we had the fish fry—do it ever year. Think grandpa just loved showin' off his wares.

It was when grandma collected all the Black Diamond rinds she would need to make her special watermelon rind preserves for the year—umm-mmm, good, yeah. They go awesome on biscuits or toast.

Grandpa loaded everbody up on the back of his old two-ton flatbed International Harvester truck an' drove down to the watermelon field. It was after we'd had breakfast an' still nice an' cool as it tended to be this time of year in the mornin's. But it would still warm up a right smart later on.

Me an' Hutch, Bobby, Don, Hubert, Jessie, an' Mister Tom piled off an' stood by the back of the truck waitin' on grandpa to give instructions on where he wanted the melons picked. He also was gonna reeducate on how to pick 'em in case anybody forgot.

Grandpa walked us all out into the field, stopped, turned around an' pointed down at a nice sized dark green Black Diamond melon.

He knelt down an' rolled it over. "Now, see here, this little curly pigtail lookin' thing on the stem?"

Everbody leaned over an' nodded. "If the melon's done growin', this curlicue withers an' turns brown...an' looky at that spot on the bottom. The darker yellow it is, the sweeter the melon is...Not quite ready if it's white or just slightly yellow...The final test is a good thump." He thumped the bottom with his big ol' finger. "Hear that hollow kinda of ring? Almost vibrates...It's ready an' it's sweet."

"Me an' Hutch's fingers are too little to do that like you do, Grandpa."

THE POND

"That's right, Foot, but you can get fair close by pokin' with the tip of your finger…like this."

He tapped it with the tip of his finger. It made almost the same sound as when he thumped it.

"Now you try it."

I bent over an' popped it with the end of my pointin' finger like a chicken peckin' in the yard—Made a fair ringin' sound.

"See?…All you kids try it."

Bobby an' them each tapped the melon. He tried to thump it like grandpa—didn't work, not enough finger.

Grandpa took out his pocket knife, jabbed it in the melon in three places, cuttin' a triangle 'bout a inch to the side. He prised the plug out with the tip of his knife. It had 'bout two inches of red meat on the bottom of the rind. The whole thing was the same length as the blade of his knife.

"Here, Foot, taste this."

I bit the end off an' looked up at grandpa. "Oh, my…that's really sweet."

"See?" He stuck the plug back in the melon.

Eatin' some melon in the field early of the mornin' when it's cool is just 'bout as good as eatin' a ripe tomater right off the vine.

"Ya'll leave the big'uns for me an' Tom. You can double up on some...Now scat, lets get this done before the sun gets too hot...They'll still be night time cool this afternoon if we get 'em in the shade up at the house quick enough."

We all scattered an' went to workin' the field an' totin' the ripe ones to the truck.

In a bit, grandpa moved us to the Charleston Gray patch, then the Crimson Sweets, an' finally, my favorite, the yella meats.

He would have a good load to take to his route customers in El Dorado tomorrow when we finished 'bout noon. Grandpa never came back from town with a single melon—ever. He even had a waitin' list.

UNION COUNTY COUNTY HOUSE

Elias Webber and Jonas Becker poured over the county maps showing who owned what in the big books they keep them in. They had several open on a large table in the County Clerk's Office.

"Here iz a Eric Hoffer..." Elias glanced at Jonas. "Zink zis could be hem using fake name?"

THE POND

"Is ze only name ve've zeen zat could be German in zis area."

"Zere is no road leading to ze property." Elias pointed at a symbol. "Could zis be a house?"

"Could be."

"But how do ve get to it?"

"Ve must go through ze John Jamison property to get zhere looks like."

The two Germans exchanged glances again.

JAMISON HOME

We took two melons of each kind an' put 'em on the tables in the shade of the sycamores at the house—grandpa parked the truck with the rest of 'em under the shade of the shed at the barn. Come 'bout 4:30 or so when daddy got here, we'd start the cuttin' an' tastin'—can't wait.

Me an' Hutch practiced with our sling shots to kill some time—he still couldn't get out of the habit of callin' 'em niggershooters, but I didn't want to hassle him 'bout it. It was his, he could call it whatever he wanted.

We collected a bunch of rocks on 'count we didn't want to lose any of our clear marbles daddy had brought us from the rig—perfect ammo for huntin' an' stuff.

Hutch picked up a sycamore ball that had fallen or maybe got shot out the tree when grandma unloaded a barrel of double ought above them German guy's heads.

"Looky here, this makes purty good ammo, too."

It wasn't late enough in for 'em to be ripe an' bust apart, they had a hard nut thing in the center. We'd sometimes even stand on the porch an' shoot 'em with daddy's .22. Had to be a fair to middlin' shot to hit one on account of they weren't quite as big as a walnut.

He put one in the leather cup, made from the tongue of an old shoe attached to two strips of innertube that were tied to each fork of the 'Y' on his shooter, pulled back an' let fly at a Calumet bakin' powder can grandma had given us we'd set on top of the fence up by the gate.

Whang! It went flyin'. "Good shot, Hutch. You've got some better."

THE POND

"Yep, have."

There was a sweet gum tree over by the tables at the side of the house where we'd put the melons. I had picked up some sweet gum balls that had opened an' already dropped most of their seeds. They were round, 'course, but were covered with what looked like little bird's mouths open for feedin' with all sorts of sharp points where the beaks would be where the seeds had been. They were a little light for shootin' very far but...

I was behind Hutch 'bout fifteen feet where he was shootin' at the bakin' powder can again. I put one of those sweet gum balls in my shooter like his, drew back an' let 'er rip. Whacked him right on the butt.

Musta stung like fire cause he jumped, rubbin' his hiney, spun around to see me gigglin' an' pointin'.

"Boy, you ought see your face."

"Dang you, Foot!" He put another sycamore ball in his pouch.

"Hey, those things are hard. No fair."

"I'll show you fair, white boy."

I took off runnin' with Hutch right behind me. Good thing he couldn't aim an' run at the same time. He tried a couple of times an' missed. Tiny was runnin' 'long side, barkin'. She thought we were playin' a game—an' I guess we were, 'cause we were best friends.

Neither one of us had time to notice the brown-eyed man squattin' in the shadows at the side of the barn laughin' at us…

§§§

CHAPTER TWELVE

JAMISON HOME

Me an' Hutch were shootin' marbles when I looked up an' saw daddy's Ford pull up out front under the sycamore.

Mama an' daddy got out the front doors an' a tall, guess you could say almost skinny girl, Hutch an' my age, got out the back door on the driver's side.

She had long bright flamin' red hair pulled back in a low pony tail. Son-of-a-gun...it was my first cousin, Frances Ann Magill. Her mama was daddy's big sister, Aunt Lollie. They lived in Kilgore, Texas—where I was born. Frances Ann's mama an' daddy, Unka Clyde, were doctors—they were both chiropractors.

Hutch nudged me. "Who's that?"

"My cousin, Frances Ann."

He looked at me. "Another cousin? How many you got?"

I shook my head. "Darned if I know, never counted 'em up."

He shook his head. "She's kinda pretty."

"Yep, she is...smart, too." I jumped up when they came through the gate an' ran over to see 'em. Tiny beat me there, though.

"Hey, Red!"

"Hey, Foot!...Hey, Tiny."

We hugged big time for 'bout five minutes. She was my favorite cousin an' the only one my same age—well, think she was seven months older'n me, but close enough.

THE POND

"This is my best friend, Hutch. Ain't his real name, but beats callin' him Seymour…Hutch, this is Frances Ann…I just call her 'Red'."

He grinned. "Wonder why?…Hidy, Red."

She stepped up an' gave him a hug, too. "Well, hidy, Hutch, friends of Foot are friends of mine, too."

He looked at me, then back at her. "Dang, Foot, she's got more freckles than you. Never thought I'd see the day…Did you walk up behind the same cow Foot did?"

Red's laugh was kinda musical. She'd heard daddy's expression 'bout walkin' up behind a cow eatin' bran an' got farted on to get my freckles—actually he usually included her.

"Oh, honey, I think I may have done it twice…" She held up two fingers. "But, my mama calls 'em sun kisses…Think the big one on the end of my nose is like Rudolph the Red Nose Reindeer in Gene Autry's song."

This time it was Hutch's turn to laugh. "Think I'm gonna like you, Red, you're funny."

"Mama always said you have to laugh at yourself first."

He nodded. "Believe I gotta agree with that."

"We share the name of one of our ancestors that signed the Declaration of Independence, Francis Lightfoot Lee, our sixth great uncle, I think...She got the Francis part, 'cept with a 'e' for a girl, an' I got the Lightfoot part...What are you doin' here, Red?"

She looked at mama an' daddy who were just standin' there grinnin' at us.

"Mama an' daddy had to go to a chiropractor convention thing in Ohio, so they sent me to stay with Uncle Joe an' Aunt Vertis while they were gone...Bus got in about noon. Aunt Vertis picked me up. Then Uncle Joe got home from work an'...here we are." She did a kind of curtsy thing. "Thank you, very much."

Guess mama told her what to wear out here on account she was wearin' blue bib overalls—the legs was cut off makin' 'em shorts like ours—an' she had a white T shirt underneath.

Daddy glanced over at the tables. "Looks like ya'll got the melons picked."

I nodded. "Yessir...Grandpa's truck's all loaded up under the shed down to the barn, too." I looked at Fran. "We get to help my grandpa haul 'em into El Dorado tomorrow to his customers. It's lots of fun."

"Oh, wow."

"But, this afternoon, we're havin' a big cuttin' an' tastin' of those over on the tables yonder that we picked this mornin'…They're still nighttime cool."

She grinned. "I love watermelon." Red looked around. "Where's Bobby?"

"Oh, him an' a couple of our other cousins are down Red Hill Road yonder…" I pointed over at it. "…fishin' for crawdads at a branch down there."

"Yum, love crawdad gumbo, too."

"If they catch enough, maybe grandma an' mama will make up a batch for supper."

"I am so goin' to enjoy bein' here."

"I'm ticlked to death you came. I've missed you a bunch."

"Missed you too, Foot."

The sheriff pulled up next to daddy's car an' him an' the doc got out. Think they were here for the cuttin' an' tastin'.

When they came in the gate, daddy introduced Frances Ann to 'em.

"Sheriff, Doc, this is my niece, Frances Ann Magill. She's here for about ten days or so while her folks are attending a convention in Ohio…They're both doctors of chiropractic in Kilgore, Texas."

Hutch nudged me an' leaned over. "What's chi-ro-practic?"

"They're doctors that make sure everthing in your back is all lined up so it all works right…Kinda like makin' sure your wirin' system don't get kinks in it."

"Oh."

I don't think he had a clue of what I just said, he just didn't want to look dumb.

"Fran, this is Sheriff Wilson and Doctor Duckworth from El Dorado."

The sheriff stuck out his hand. "Happy to meet you, Frances."

The doc smiled big an' also shook her hand. He glanced at me, then back at her. "I can certainly see the resemblance…same eyes."

"An' freckles…'cept more of 'em."

He looked down at Hutch an' nodded. "That too."

Fran punched his shoulder. "Ow."

He rubbed it, but didn't punch her back. Figured that would come later.

"Betcha ya'll are here for the melons, ain'tcha?"

The sheriff grinned. "How'd you guess, Foot?"

I glanced at daddy. "Just a SWAG."

Daddy laughed an' looked at the sheriff. "Something he got from me, Myron...Scientific wild-assed guess."

It was mama's turn to do the thumpin', which she did with her elbow. "Robert Reese!...It didn't need to be explained."

The sheriff arched his eyebrows. "Well, I wasn't sure, Vertis."

Grandma stepped out on the porch—grandpa was just behind her.

"Well don't ya'll stand out in the yard all day, come on up here on the porch...and who is that gorgeous child?"

We all walked up to the porch an' climbed the steps to the stoop.

"Grandma, Grandpa, this is my most favorite cousin from Texas, Frances Ann. Her mama's daddy's big sister...I just call her Red."

She curtsied again in front of grandma. "I'm please to meet you, ma'am."

"Oh, you can call me Grandma like the rest of the kids around here...You're one of the bunch, now."

"Yes, ma'am...uh, Grandma."

Hutch kinda beamed in that he got to talk. "I call her Miz Mame an' Foot's grandpa, Mister John on account of I'm different."

Grandma glanced down at him an' caressed the side of his face. "Hutch, honey, you can call me Grandma, too, if you're a mind too. It would be fine with me." She winked at him.

I think he nearly teared up at that. He nodded but looked like he was a little choked 'cause he didn't say nothin'.

Grandpa stepped down the stoop an' headed toward the tables in the shade where the melons were. "Well, now that everybody's here, we just as well get started with this year's cuttin' an' tastin'....Vertis, you mind going inside and gettin' a butcher knife?"

"Okay, Daddy, be right back." Mama opened the screen door an' stepped inside the house.

THE POND

Grandpa pulled out his Barlow foldin' knife. He always cut the first one, a Black Diamond, with it. He would slice it all the way around from top to bottom, then hit the cut with his big ol' ham-like fist to bust it open. It always pulled the heart up so he could cut a chunk off. Grandpa got the first bite.

He stuck it in his mouth an' chewed once. It didn't take much. Grandpa swallowed, turned an' looked at everbody, nodded, an' held up his thumb.

We all clapped at the ceremony as mama came back out with grandma's long butcher knife an' some towels for everbody to wipe their hands an' faces with—we tended to get kinda messy. She also had some bib things grandma had made for those who wanted 'em.

Grandpa started cuttin' slices from the melon an' grandma passed them around. There wadn't no eatin' utensils, you had to hold the slice up an' take a bite—um-mmmm.

While he was cuttin', I just happened to turn an' out of the corner of my eye, saw the figure of a man squattin' in the shadow of the barn, just watchin' us. Kinda had an idea who it was, but figured he didn't want nobody to know he was there, so I didn't say nothin.

Red got her slice right before Hutch. She took a big bite right out of the middle, looked up at grandpa with those bright blue eyes of hers that were near big as saucers.

"Oh, my, my, my, Grandpa, this is almost decadent."

Now I didn't have no idea what decadent was, but figured from her expression it was better'n good.

"Thank you, Frances, glad you like it. I've been growing these Black Diamonds for over forty years."

She grinned. "You can call me Fran like my daddy does...Grandpa."

He nodded. "All right, Fran."

Grandpa had cut both Black Diamonds an' the Charleston Grays, then started on the Crimson Sweets.

Everbody oooed an' ahhhhed over the taste an' sweetness. Even Tiny was dancin' in circles for her piece—she loved watermelon, too.

THE POND

Mama looked up at grandpa, even she had juice runnin' down her chin. That happens when you just had to dive in a slice an' start eating in the middle.

"Oh, goodness, Papa, these are marvelous...best ever."

Everbody was noddin' their heads as they looked up from their own slice.

"Don't ya'll get cocky yet, I'm fixin' to cut my yella meats. Been special growing them for almost ten years now."

Hutch was the first in line, 'cause he was first to finish his slice of Crimson Sweet. He got his yella meat, took a monstrous bite out of the middle, an' I kid you not, promptly dropped to his hiney an' fell on his back.

Red bent over him. "Hutch, you okay?"

"Think I died an went to Heaven." He sat up an' looked at Grandpa. "Gol-uh-olee, Mister John."

Everbody was crowdin' up to get their slice an' the response was almost the same. Oh, nobody else fell down, but you could still tell they were blown away with the taste.

Bobby, Don, an' Hubert had showed up just as grandpa was cuttin' the Sweets, they had 'bout half a bucket of crawdads. They'd have to clean 'em after the cuttin' an' tastin'. Grandma said she'd start the gumbo soon as they were done.

'Bout another ten minutes later, everbody had finished their slices of the yella meats an' were pattin' their stomachs.

Grandma wiped her hands an' face an' looked at the grownups. "I got the coffee on, ya'll come inside, I'm sure it's ready."

The sheriff wiped his face, too. "Sounds good, Mame, could use a cup now."

All the grownups got cleaned up an' headed inside. Bobby an' them went to the cleanin' table near the back kitchen door to take care of all them crawdads.

I leaned over to Fran an' Hutch. "Think I'm fixin' to go get in some trouble...Ya'll in?"

Hutch grinned an' nudged Fran. "This is probably goin' to be good, Red."

She nodded. "Lead on, O mighty one...Hadn't been in trouble since I left Texas."

I stepped over to the table, got a slice of Sweet, handed it to Fran, an' I got a slice of yella meat.

"Carry this...Let's go."

THE POND

I led the way through the gate toward the barn. Tiny padded 'longside.

Fran moved up beside me. "What do you have in mind, Foot?"

I glanced at her. "You'll see."

§§§

CHAPTER THIRTEEN

HAYNESVILLE ROAD

"Vhere are zhose kids going?"

Elias turned the focus knob on the field glasses. "Zhey're carrying some vatermelon out to ze barn."

"Vhy?"

He looked at Jonas and shrugged. "Maybe to give to ze mule."

Jonas nodded. "Maybe…Vonder who ze redheaded girl child is vhat came mit ze white boy's parents?"

Elias shook his head and brought the glasses back to his eyes.

"I zink ve zhould keep a closer eye on ze kids rather zan ze grandfather…*Ja*?"

Elias lowered the binoculars again. "*Ja*…Maybe harder zince the kids vonder around playing."

"Maybe."

JAMISON HOME

I eased up to the corner of the barn an' peeked around to the back side. The man that had been squattin' in the shadows on the side had moved around to the back—guess when he saw us comin'. He was standin' with his back to the wall, kinda plastered up against it.

I looked at him. "You're Unka Dud, ain'tcha?"

"Didn't zink anyone zaw me."

"Kinda did outta the corner of my eye. Mister Tom says you can see things that ain't supposed to be there by not lookin' at 'em."

Hutch looked at me. "Huh?…That makes no sense at all."

Fran nodded. "Well, yes it does, Hutch. If you try to focus on something, your eyes can lie to you, but if you don't…they can't."

"What?"

"Brought you some of grandpa's watermelon." I handed him the slice I carried. "This one is a Crimson Sweet an' my cousin, Red, here, has a slice of yella meat for you…Figured you didn't want grandpa or Sheriff Wilson to know you was here, so I didn't tell 'em."

He nodded an' took a bite of the Sweet, then looked back over at me an' the others. "Oh, my, my, my, this iz zweet, isn't it. Zhank you. I vas getting a little hungry."

"Thought you might…Oh, this is my best friend, Hutch, an' this is my favorite cousin just in from Texas for a visit, Frances Ann…I just call her, Red."

Unka Dud smiled. "I zhought as much…Knew vho Hutch vas, but not Frances…Is nice to meet you…Actually Uncle Dud vas a name zome of the local children gave me years ago vhen I ztarted letting zem zwim and fish in my pond. My name iz

Eric…but Uncle Dud is fine." He ate some more melon.

"I knew your name was Eric Hoffer on account of I heard grandpa mention it…when me an' Hutch found the…"

He looked up from the melon an' wiped his chin with the back of his sleeve. "Skull…I know."

"You knew?"

"I vatched you from the woods, zhen I vatched while you and Tom Rayford brought up ze rest of ze bones and other skull…I vondered if anyone vould ever find zem."

Fran frowned an' looked at me. "Skulls?…Bones? What is it that I don't know?"

She punched my arm—hard. "You better start talkin', Foot."

"Zhey found two skeletons in my pond…I put zem zere over zhirty-five years ago."

"That's why the sheriff wants to talk to you."

He nodded. "I know…but I am not ready to talk about it. Now iz not ze time."

"It's those two guys from Germany, ain't it?"

He wiped his mouth again an' nodded. "I don't vant zem to know vhere I am…Ze vould do me harm. I have zomething zhey vant…badly."

"Figured…Me an' Hutch put both of 'em on their butts…They were carryin' guns, those German Luger kind."

"I know, I zaw."

Fran punched my arm. "You did what?"

I turned to her. "Me an' Hutch been learnin' some stuff called Judo…formed a club. They tried to grab us to make us talk, but weren't nice about it. We used some stuff we'd been practicin' on 'em."

"Really? Can I join and learn it?"

"Sure, Red, we practice a lot. Only learned two Judo moves so far, though…But we'll add another when the next issue of *Judo Joe* comic book comes out…"

"Comic book?"

"Uh-huh…Better close your mouth 'fore a fly finds it."

She snapped her mouth shut with a pop, but her eyes didn't change.

I took the Sweet rind from Unka Dud an' nodded at Fran to hand him the yella meat. "We'll put these rinds in Sally's feed trough."

Fran looked at me. "Sally?"

"Grandma's milk cow…she likes the rinds, but so does Ted."

THE POND

She shook her head. "Ted?"

"Grandpa's Tennessee plow mule...We'll take the wheelbarrow back to the yard to get all the other rinds from the cuttin' an' tastin' an' bring 'em back out here for Sally an' Ted...in case anybody asks what we were doin' out here."

"Good thinkin'."

I looked at Hutch. "I know."

He thumped me an' so did Fran. Unka Dud just grinned as he looked up from eatin' on the yella meat.

I wadn't gonna ask why them fellas wanted to hurt him. The fact that he was kinda 'fraid of 'em was good enough for me...Figured he wanted us to know, he'd a told us.

He handed me the yella meat rind. I ran inside the barn through the double doors on the back side an' chunked the two rinds in Sally's trough. She was already standin in it ready for her evenin' feed an' milkin'—she started crunchin' on 'em right away.

"Zank you for ze vatermelon. I vill slip back across ze pasture now."

"Make sure you can't be seen from the Haynesville Road. Them fellas been parkin' up the way a piece in a black Ford an' watchin' the house with binoculars thinkin' grandpa an' the sheriff will lead them to you."

"Zank you. Iz goot information to have." He nodded an' headed off, keepin' the barn 'tween him an' the road. To be 'round grandpa's age, he moved real smooth an' quiet, sorta like a cat.

I looked at Hutch an' Fran. "Ya'll ready to head back to the house?"

She nodded. "Probably should."

"You grab the wheelbarrow over yonder, Hutch." I pointed inside to just off the wide aisleway in the barn.

"What's the matter, you don't know nothin' 'bout machinery?"

"Well, yeah, but you're closer."

"Oh, right."

"I'll get the front doors...Red, why don't you get the gate at the yard."

"I can do that."

We pushed the wheelbarrow 'cross the sand road in front of grandpa's house that led down to Unka JB's.

THE POND

HAYNESVILLE ROAD

"Zo, vhat are zey doing now?"

Jonas looked away from the glasses. "Taking ze vheelbarrow into ze yard. Apparently to get ze vatermelon rinds."

"Vonder vhat took zem zo long?"

Jonas shook his head. "Maybe ze were sneaking off to have ze smoke. I am told American children vill do zat."

Elias nodded. "*Ja*."

JAMISON HOME

"Well, you kids read my mind. I appreciate you bringin' the wheelbarrow."

Grandpa looked up from where he was at the tables with daddy an' Mister Tom. They were sortin' the seeds from the different types of melons we had sampled for dryin'. He always saved the seed from the cuttin' an' tastin' each year for plantin' next year—he picked the best ones to bring up for tastin'.

Hutch parked the wheelbarrow next to the tables an' me, Red, an' him started chunkin' the rinds an' left over melon slices grandpa was done gettin' the seeds from in it. Sally an' Ted was sure gonna have a feast this evenin'.

We filled up the wheelbarrow, could tell it was gonna take 'least two trips. I went to grab the handles an' Mister Tom stepped in.

"Here, let me push that, Foot. It's pretty heavy and wheelbarrows are not known to be real stable if you get it off balance when they're full."

"Okay, we'll go with you an' help unload the stuff in Sally an' Ted's feed troughs."

Mister Tom leaned down as we went out the gate an' toward the barn. "Did Uncle Dud enjoy those slices of melon ya'll took out there?"

I swallowed hard an' looked in his eyes. Know mine were big as softballs. "Uh…"

He smiled. "Yeah, I saw him, too. Could tell he didn't want to talk to the sheriff right now. Ya'll did good."

I glanced back over my shoulder to make sure grandpa an' them couldn't hear us. "Yessir, an' you're right, he don't want to talk yet…knows 'bout those two German fellas. Says they want somethin' he's got an' will hurt 'im to get it."

He nodded. "Figured it was something like that."

"Said he put those bodies in his pond over thirty-five years ago…Didn't ask 'im why an' he didn't offer to say nothin' else."

"He's a really nice man."

Mister Tom glanced at Fran an' nodded. "I haven't talked to him in years."

Fran moved up close to us as Hutch opened the front barn doors so Mister Tom could push the wheelbarrow through.

"I think he's kinda lonely."

He set the wheelbarrow down so me an' Hutch could start takin' the rinds out, breakin' 'em in two pieces, an' throwin' 'em into the troughs—knew grandma or grandpa would be out in a bit to milk Sally. She'd be real content by then after eatin' all that watermelon.

Mister Tom glanced at Fran. "Think so?"

"Uh-huh. Don't really believe he wanted to go back to his cabin yet…Foot told him about those men watching the house, so he made sure he stayed out of sight."

"Could well be, Red. He's been out at his cabin alone for a long time…I'm positive he knows he's a wanted man…but I don't think it's by the law in the United States."

§§§

CHAPTER FOURTEEN

EL DORADO, ARK

Jonas pulled into the curb in front of the Western Union office across the street from the court house and parked.

"I vill go inzide and zend zhat telegram ve talked about."

"Zen ve go get zomething to eat before ve go to ze motel, *ja*?"

Jonas nodded at Elias. "*Ja*, ve eat, zen go rest, and vait."

JAMISON HOME

After supper of the gumbo an' cornbread grandma had promised to make of the crawdads Bobby an' them caught, me, Fran, an' Hutch were sittin' out in the yard countin' fireflies.

"That was wonderful apple pie with that big dollop of butter meltin' on top, wasn't it?"

I smiled. "Most everthin' grandma fixes is wonderful, Red."

She nodded. "Wouldn't doubt it…Wouldn't doubt it at all."

The grownups were on the porch havin' their after dinner coffee. Don an' Hubert had already walked up to their house just a hunderd yards up the road. Bobby was on the porch havin' a cup of coffee, too—actin' like he was one of the grownups since he was now a teenager.

Daddy got to his feet. "Well, John, Mame, sure enjoyed the melons an' the gumbo, but it's about time we went home. Have to get up at five to get ready to head out to the rig."

Mama also stood an' turned to Bobby. "Are you staying out here with Foot?"

He shook his head. "No, Mama, think I'll go home…got some things I want to do in town tomorrow."

Bobby was sweet on a girl from his class that lived just across the street from us.

"Frances, are you ready to go?"

"Can I stay out here with Foot, Aunt Vertis?…Is that all right, Grandma?"

"Of course, child, as long as it's okay with Vertis and Joe."

Mama cut a glance at daddy, then back to Fran. "Honey, you know my mama an' daddy don't have electricity or runnin' water out here like we do in town…You're not used to that."

"Oh, that's okay, Aunt Vertis, I don't mind." She looked at me an' Hutch. "If they can handle it…so can I. We've got a contest going on countin' fireflies."

Daddy grinned an' shook his head. "Just don't tell Lollie that you spent the night where there wasn't electricity or indoor bathroom facilities, she'll have my hide."

She giggled. "I know...Not to worry, Uncle Joe. I do know you an' mama or my other aunts an' uncles didn't have electricity or runnin' water out at the home place back where ya'll grew up in Navarro County."

He nodded. "Got a point there, girl...Okay, we'll be back out tomorrow when I get home from work."

Mama, Daddy, an' Bobby waved bye as they drove off an' me, Hutch, an' Red went back to our countin' fireflies.

Grandma got up from her rocker. "I'll go make you boys your pallets on the back porch. Frances, I'll turn down your covers in the bedroom across the hall from ours. Ya'll can turn in whenever you're ready."

Fran looked up from where we were sittin' out in the yard. "Grandma, can I sleep out on the porch on a pallet with Foot an' Hutch?"

She shook her head an' frowned. "Well, I suppose so, but why do you want to sleep on that old hard floor instead of a nice featherbed?"

Fran glanced at me. "Foot says they can see shootin' stars an' watch the moon come up from back there...He an' Hutch told me that if they hadn't been sleepin' out there last year with Tiny, that Cobb man would have set fire to the house and burned up everyone inside."

Grandma nodded. "I suppose that's true."

"Besides it's kinda like camping out...without the bugs." Fran slapped a mosquito on her arm.

Grandma shook her head an' grinned as she opened the screen door. "You kids."

In a bit, grandpa got up an' headed inside to go to bed an' Mister Tom took off walkin' the short mile down the dirt road to his place. The sheriff an' Doc Duckworth drove off toward El Dorado—they offered Mister Tom a ride but he said he enjoyed a good walk in the dark after supper. Then grandma came back out on the porch.

"All right, children, your pallets are ready and there's a lamp on the little table by the wall. Just lower the wick way down when you turn in...and don't be talking all night. We'll be gettin' up at daylight."

We replied pretty much in unison as we got to our feet an' brushed off our fannies. "Yessum."

When we got to our pallets down at the end of the dog run an' laid down, I noticed Tiny didn't waste no time in gettin' 'tween me an' Fran. She promptly planted her head on Fran's leg, took a deep breath an' let it all out, like dogs do when they're content an' relaxin'.

Hutch turned his head toward me. "You know, Foot, we oughta make Red a niggershooter like ours tomorrow."

Fran glanced at him. "A what?"

"Slingshot, you know...wrist rocket? Can't get him outta the habit of callin' it a niggershooter...done it all his life. He don't mean nothin' by it."

I could see her shakin' her head an' shrug her shoulders. "Oh, okay."

"Me an' Foot will show you how to shoot one tomorrow after we do the practice session on our judo stuff."

"Daddy brings clear marbles in from the rig an' we use 'em for ammo...Them,'mong other things."

Could tell that Fran turned her blue eyes to me. "What do you mean, 'other things'?"

"Well, sometimes whatever's handy...hickory nuts, acorns, pecans, rocks, sycamore balls, sweet gum balls, an' such...Work purty good, don't they, Hutch?"

THE POND

Couldn't see nothin' but the whites of his eyes as he glared at me in the near darkness—I giggled.

"What's funny?"

I leaned over toward Fran. "I shot him in the butt with a sweet gum ball...they're kinda prickly."

Hutch reached over an' whacked me on the stomach. I giggled again—she joined me.

Guess Fran musta been tired from the trip an' all 'cause I didn't hear nothin' else from her or Tiny but soft an' steady breathin'—think the sandman slipped up on the both of 'em. They'll probably write a song 'bout that one day.

Errr-er-rrr-er-rrr! Rosco greeted the rosy glow just showin' at the far eastern horizon.

Fran jerked bolt upright on her pallet. "What? What? Who?"

She glanced around kinda frightened on account she didn't know what the sound was that woke her up. Then the big Road Island Red rooster of grandpa's did it again.

Fran looked outside at the early mornin' light an' could make him out on top of the picket fence that went around the yard. He fluffed his feathers, flapped his wings a couple times, an' greeted the mornin' sun once again.

I rolled over an' looked up at her. "Name's Rosco. He thinks the sun comes up just to hear him crow."

"My Lord, he's just outside the door."

"Yeah, it's sorta right between the chicken coop where his ladies are an' the house. He's tellin' everbody it's time to get up an' get to doin'."

"Really?"

"Yep, does it ever mornin'." I pointed outside in the yard. "See...His ladies are already comin' out, scratchin' an' peckin' for any worms that hadn't gone back under ground yet. Grandma will be out there with their scratch after she starts the fire in her stove."

"Every morning?"

"Uh-huh."

Fran flopped back down an' buried her face in her feather pillow. I looked over an' Hutch hadn't moved yet—he's a real slow starter. Looks like my cuz ain't a whole lots faster.

Grandma was comin' down the big hallway carryin' a kerosene lantern headed to the kitchen. She saw I was awake.

"Figured you'd be awake, Foot. Looks like Hutch or Frances aren't quite with us yet."

I grinned. "Rosco near made Fran wet her pallet with his first crow. She threw herself back down when she found out that it was a rooster that noise was...City girl."

"Suspect we'll break her in to the country if she stays long enough."

Grandma disappeared into the kitchen an' lit another couple of lamps, then I could hear her puttin' kindlin' in her cook stove an' light it with some wadded up newspaper. She'd be goin' out to the hen house in a minute.

Grandpa would go out to the woods pretty regular an' find an' old dead pine that's fallen. He'd bust everthing away, but the heart, which was bright yellow, near pure pitch, an' bring it back to split up into slivers for the kindling—would catch in a heartbeat.

Figured I'd go ahead an' get up, see as she needed any help—need to make my mornin' call to the outhouse anyways.

After the mornin' chores had been done, everbody was up an' sittin' 'round the table havin' breakfast.

Grandma fixed one of my favorite breakfasts, biscuits an' venison sausage gravy. Don't think Fran ever had it before, ate more'n me an' Hutch put together. She liked grandma's buttermilk, too.

We'd go outside after breakfast an' do our judo practice an' bring her up to snuff. Then we'd make her that sling shot an' teach her how to shoot it. Gonna be a fun day.

SPRING MOTEL, EL DORADO

A knock sounded on the door of the room in the one-story, U shaped motel on the outskirts of El Dorado. Elias opened it to see a messenger in a dark green uniform and a military parade type short billed hat.

"Telegram for Mister Becker."

"I'll take it." Elias handed the young man a quarter after he got the yellow missive.

The teenager looked at the coin in his hand and frowned. "Thank you, sir. Will there be a reply?"

THE POND

Elias glanced back at Jonas who shook his head. "No, zhank you." He closed the door in the boy's face before he had a chance to respond or even turn around.

Jonas got up from where he was sitting on the edge of the bed, took the telegram and opened it. He looked up at Elias when he finished reading the short flimsy and nodded.

§§§

CHAPTER FIFTEEN

JAMISON HOME

"Ahhh!" Hutch rolled back an' forth tryin' to catch his breath.

Fran bent over him an' looked into his rapidly blinkin' dark brown eyes. "You okay, Hutch?"

He finally took a couple of deep breaths an' nodded. Tiny walked up an' sniffed him. Guess to see if he was still alive or not.

Fran held out her hand an' helped him up. "Sorry, didn't mean to throw you down so hard."

Hutch put his hands on his knees an' took a few more breaths, then straightened up. "That's okay. You're really quick...lots faster'n me or Foot."

Fran kinda blushed under her freckles an' looked at her bare feet. "I have a confession." She raised her eyes an' glanced at the both of us. "I've been takin' tumbling back in Kilgore. Can tell right off that it really helps in this judo stuff...Is that all ya'll have, those two throws?"

"So far...There's a sort of a preview of next month's lesson here in the back behind all the pictures."

"What is it?"

I turned to Hutch. "Near as I can tell if somebody reaches out to grab you that's lots bigger, it's a way to handle that situation."

I motioned for Hutch to come closer. He shook his head.

"Uh-uh...Try it on Red. I gotta rest a minute."

"Titti-baby...Okay, cuz, here's the deal. Somebody reaches out atcha, you grab the front of their shirt or coat, fall backwards to your back..."

"Hey, wait a minute." Hutch pointed down on the ground. "They'll fall on top of you."

I shook my head. "Nope...'Cause as you fall back, you bring your knee to your chest an' put your foot in their stomach...Now, it says to keep hold of their shirt an' shove with your leg, hard."

"Oh, I see. Their momentum of fallin' with you holdin' on to their shirt an' kickin' with your leg, throws them over you to land on their back."

I nodded. "You got it, Red."

"Let me do it first."

"Okay."

I started to reach for her an' the next thing I knew, I was lookin' at the sky an' landin' on my back, behind her head. *Whoosh, oof!* All the air came out of my lungs like it did Hutch's a minute ago.

She jumped to her feet just by kickin' both legs in the air in one smooth motion, then spun around lookin' down at me.

"Oops, sorry, Foot, didn't realize you'd go so far...that one's really neat." She helped me up like she did Hutch.

"Boy, Red, you take to this like a duck to water."

"It's really fun. I'll have mama see if anyone in Kilgore or Longview teaches it when I go back home."

Hutch looked over at me. "Hope me an' you survive her visit."

I nodded. "Yeah, got that right...What say we go see as we can find the right branch to make her slingshot with?"

"I'm for that."

Fran looked at both of us. "Is that all the practicin' we're going to do today?"

"Uh, I think so...You, Hutch?"

"Uh-huh."

Me an' Fran shook the sand off the old quilt grandma let us have to practice on, folded it up an' laid it inside the back door. Grandma said she had a place to keep it for us.

We headed across the road at the side of the house to grandpa's truck garden. There was a big grove of trees just beyond it that went all the way down the hill to the Yankee meadow.

Right away, Tiny went to sniffin' about the bushes in the woods for coon scat or rabbit pee.

"What kind of tree are we lookin' for?"

"I'd say a young hickory or pecan, wouldn't you, Hutch?"

"Uh-huh."

I pulled my slingshot out an' showed Fran the kind an' size of fork we'd be lookin' for.

"Think yours can be the same size as mine an' Hutch's."

"Oh, okay. I see…What about those rubber straps an' that little piece of leather?"

"There's what's left of an old inner tube out in the barn from grandpa's truck. Me an' Hutch cut ours from it…Have to see if grandma has any old shoes anywhere from when mama's brothers were kids…She never throws away nothin'."

"Shoes?"

I showed her my sling shot again. "This leather piece that we put the ammo in is from the tongue of an old shoe."

"So you just punch a hole in each end to tie those rubber straps through?"

"'Bout the size of it."

"Think I see a possibility, ya'll." Hutch pointed at a fork with fairly equal branches comin' off at the right angles.

THE POND

"Could be, Hutch." I looked at Fran. "Red, wrap your hand around this part here, see how it fits."

She grabbed it, glanced back at me an' nodded. "Feels good."

I took my Barlow out opened the spey blade an' notched the branch just below the bottom of her hand. Daddy had showed me how to sharpen my blades so that any of the three would shave—not that I needed to yet, but that's how sharp they were.

"Okay, you can let go."

She released her grip an' stepped back. I walked my blade completely around the branch several times, mashin' it deeper each time. After the third pass, I nodded to Hutch. "Pop that sucker off, right there."

He grabbed above an' below my groove an' gave it a hard twistin' snap with his top hand—broke right off.

I took it an' cleaned up the bottom of the cut so there weren't any splinters, then went to work on the forks. Didn't take no time atall till Hutch could snap each one of them off an' I could smooth them up, too.

I also peeled the bark away from the top inch on each fork where we'd be tyin' the rubber strips. That bark'll dry over time an' the strips can slip off.

I held it up to Fran. "Here you go, Red, now we go back to the house. Think grandma has an old pair of scissors we can use to cut the inner tube with…She ain't about to let us use her good sewin' scissors to cut no rubber with."

When we walked into the kitchen, grandma was strainin' the mornin's fresh milk to get any hairs or flies out that might have fallen in while milkin'.

"Grandma, do you have an old pair of scissors we could borrow to cut some strips of inner tube for Fran's sling shot?"

She looked at us over the top of her wire-rimmed glasses for a couple seconds. "Oh, I expect I do." Grandma opened a drawer in the cabinet an' took a pair of long ones out. "I use these to cut chicken joints apart, so bring 'em back so I can wash them up."

"Yessum…Oh, where's grandpa?"

"He's down plowin' up some old corn stalks with Ted so he can plant some fall greens. He'll be in shortly.

We turned to leave.

THE POND

"And don't run with them."

"No, ma'am."

I went in the tack room an' got the old inner tube from grandpa's International Harvester flat bed.

There were several patches on it an' we couldn't use those areas. Me an' Hutch made new ones last year an' it had already been cut in two.

"Here, Hutch, hold this end…tight." I held the other end an' we stretched it out straight.

"What do you think, 'bout fourteen, fifteen inches?"

He nodded. "That'll give us enough on the ends to tie to the tops of the forks an' still have a good twelve inches left."

"My thinkin', too."

I went to cuttin' the first strap, 'bout a half-inch wide with grandma's scissors. Snipped it off at near fifteen inches, an' then cut another just like it.

There was a roll of fishin' line in the tack room. We got that an' grandpa's leather punch.

I handed them to Fran. "Here, Red, you tote these."

We went back inside to see 'bout a couple old shoes.

"Here's your scissors, Grandma…didn't hurt 'em none…don't think."

She reached for 'em. "You weren't cutting wire or anything like that, were you?"

"Oh, no, ma'am, just cuttin' on an old inner tube…Reckon you got a pair of wore-out shoes that Unka Dorris or Unka Rube or any of 'em might have worn?…We need a tongue."

She nodded an' wiped her hands on a dish towel. "Ah, of course you do…Ya'll come on."

We followed her back to the small bedroom next to hers an' grandpa's where me an' Bobby slept sometimes. There was a little closet in there. She opened it an' found a pair of brogans with holes in the soles.

"Here, these were your Uncle Ellis's." She handed me one. "One reason why I save stuff. Now, ya'll scat, I still have work to do."

"Thanks, Grandma." Fran gave her a big hug.

She swatted her behind with her dish towel she was still holdin'. "Oh, get out of here."

We went out to the front porch an' sat on the edge. Tiny was right beside us like she'd been all mornin'.

THE POND

I handed the shoe she gave me to Hutch to cut the tongue off an' shape it up with his pocket knife.

When he finished that, I gave it to Fran. "Okay, you take this an' put holes in each end with the biggest punch on this wheel."

I took the leather punch, rolled the wheel around to the biggest one an' handed it to her. It was a little less than a quarter inch.

I folded one strap around the top of a fork an' held it with my fingers. "Okay, Hutch, you know the routine, wrap this fishin' line 'bout a dozen times 'round close up next to the fork…tight as you can pull it while I hold it."

"I know, I know…Quit bein' so bossy."

"Wadn't bein' bossy."

"Were too."

"Was not."

"Were too."

"Was not."

"Would ya'll hush…Good gosh, sound like children."

Fran just shook her head as she put the end of the tongue between the punch wheel an' the base an' squeezed the handle, puttin' a nice round hole in it.

We hushed, got both straps tied on an' she handed me the leather tongue with the holes in each end.

I worked the rubber strap through the hole, folded it back on itself just like on the top of the fork an' Hutch tied it off the same way.

I held it up. "Bingo! Here you go, Red. You are now armed."

"Wow, thanks ya'll. Guess now we practice?"

SPRING MOTEL, EL DORADO

The afternoon sun was nearing the horizon when a new 1950 dark green Packard sedan pulled into the central open area of the motel.

It parked in front of Room #5. Four men in various dark shades of blue and brown suits, all wearing fedora type felt hats, got out.

One of the men knocked on the door. Elias opened it. The four men removed their hats and stepped inside.

§§§

CHAPTER SIXTEEN

JAMISON HOME

We finished breakfast of buttermilk pancakes with butter an' sorghum an' bacon before we headed out to grandpa's truck.

"We'll get some more practice in with your slingshot when we get back from helpin' grandpa deliver his melons, Red."

"That's okay, Foot. My wrist was a little sore this morning anyway."

Hutch grinned. "Yeah, can get that way…musta shot forty or fifty rocks an' nuts yesterday."

"When do I get to try the marbles?"

Me an' Hutch exchanged glances.

"When you get a bit better at hittin' your target so's we don't lose the marbles…They're primo ammo."

Hutch frowned an' turned to me as we got to the truck. "What's 'primo'?"

"Means 'top quality'…the best."

Fran beat me to the answer.

"Saw it in a book and looked it up…You need to read more, Hutch."

"Ain't got no books."

"Is there a library in your town?"

"Yeah, but coloreds ain't allowed in it."

I shook my head. "That's about the dumbest thing I ever heard…I got a bunch at home. I'll loan 'em to you…But you better take care of 'em. No dog-eared pages."

"What's dog-eared?"

Fran opened the passenger door. "Turnin' down the corner of a page to keep your place."

THE POND

"How do you keep it, then?"

"With a piece of ribbon or a slip of paper between the pages."

"Huh…that's a neat idea."

She smiled. "I thought it was."

Hutch nodded, looked at me, nodded his head and grinned. "Yep, your cousin awright."

Fran punched his arm. "Hey, what does that mean?"

"Huh? Oh, nothin'…just commentin'."

Grandpa got in an' slammed his door. "All right, Frances, keep your legs on that side of the gear shift lever. I'll be shifting up and down when we start off an' slow down."

"I know, Grandpa. I've ridden in trucks."

"Then, we're off."

He stepped on the starter button on the floor next to the accelerator an' the old truck turned over several times an' roared to life. Grandpa shifted back into low an' eased out on the clutch as we pulled away from the house toward the Haynesville Road an' headed to El Dorado. He shifted the long lever into second, an' then third when we hit the blacktop.

EAST SIDE CAFE

Six men exited the cafe after having breakfast and coffee. The leader of the new men that had come in last evening from Dallas, Amell Schmidt, turned to Jonas.

"How long have you and Elias been here eating zis vhat ze Americans call breakfast?"

Jonas turned to him as they walked back to the Spring Motel next door. "Two veeks now. You vill get used to it."

"No Brötchen rolls, or even rye bread. Yust zat tasteless vhite bread…toasted. No bratvurst. Zheir zausage here is bland…zheir jam vas goot, though."

"True, and ze coffee is tolerable…a little veek, but drinkable."

"Vhere can ve get some goot German beer?"

Jonas glanced at Elias.

"At zheir stores zat zell only liquor. Ze do have Becks."

Elias nodded. "But ze zell it cold. Ve set it out in our room to varm up zo it is acceptable."

They entered Jonas and Elias' room.

THE POND

"*Ja*, goot…Ve vill study ze local maps and make plans…Ve must find zat Gypsy Jew Motshan Beiler and ze treasure his organization stole from us zirty-five years ago…Ze Fourth Reich needs it for our new Fuehrer in Argentina."

Grandpa pulled up to the front of May's Cafe to get us some hamburgers an' Nehi Orange drinks. She'd quit sayin' anything 'bout servin' coloreds in her place—knew better than to mess with grandpa.

Besides we were goin' to eat 'em in the truck on the way back to the house anyhow.

It didn't take no time atall to get rid of all the watermelons. Grandpa's customers knew how good they were. The Cooks were havin' a family reunion this weekend at the city park an' they took the most of 'em.

Good thing the three of us weren't grownups, we'd a never fit in the front seat of grandpa's truck.

As it was, each of us held our Nehi's between our legs—they were cold, too. An' we unwrapped an' ate the hamburgers—were sure good, too. Grandpa could do it with one hand, don't know how, but he did.

"What are you scamps going to get into this afternoon?"

Fran glanced over at grandpa. "Grandma asked me to pick some dewberries for a cobbler. Said there was some vines down toward..." She turned to me. "What do you call it, Foot...Yankee meadow?"

"Yep...The vines are there back this side of the meadow just a ways in the woods. Want me an' Hutch to come along?"

"No, think I'll walk down there an' practice with my new slingshot on the way...That's the best way, I think, rather that shootin' at cans on the fence...Besides, my wrist is feeling some better."

"Gotta agree with that, Red. We're gonna go over an' help Mister Tom carry some more apples back for grandma's root cellar...Oughta be back 'bout the same time."

Grandpa pulled the truck into the shed next to the barn. We all piled out an' ran to the yard.

Tiny was spinnin' 'round in circles just inside the gate—happy to see us back. Didn't seem to matter if we were gone most of the day, or five minutes, She was happy to see us an' always showed it.

THE POND

Tiny jumped all the way from the ground up into Fran's arms an' went to kissin' on her. She seemed to take to girls like she did Ellie—the girl we rescued last year from that killer preacher.

Fran set her down on the porch after we climbed the steps. Me an' Hutch took on off toward Mister Tom's, looked like Tiny was gonna stay with Fran an' go down berry pickin' with her—an' that was okay. It was a pretty good run for her over to Mister Tom's, 'sides, she loved to run through the woods sniffin' for critters.

"How full do you want me to get this lard bucket, Grandma?" She held up the gallon bucket.

"Oh, I would think about half to three-quarters would be plenty, honey…Get those big ripe ones, they'll be closer to the plant. The ones out on the end of the vine are the last to ripen."

Fran nodded. "Yes, ma'am, I know. Be back in a little bit…Come on, Tiny."

They walked down the Red Hill Road, Fran picked up little rocks along the way and practiced shooting at trees and occasionally at a squirrel running along a branch—and missing.

She and Tiny cut off the road toward where Foot said the vines were and found them in short order near a game trail.

After sticking the slingshot in her back pocket, she started picking the biggest she could find—after eating a couple.

"Umm, sweet. Too bad you don't like 'em, Tiny."

Thirty minutes later, her bucket was almost half full of big, juicy berries. Tiny turned and faced the game trail that led up from the meadow and growled. The hair on her back stood up.

Frances looked up to see two men in khaki pants and shirts approaching.

"Who are you?"

"It does not matter little girl, you are coming mit us."

She set her bucket down and started backing away shaking her head. Tiny lunged at the nearest of the two men and grabbed his pant leg in her teeth, snarling and jerking at the material.

The second man picked up a broken branch from the ground and swung it like a baseball player.

He knocked the little dog rolling, finally coming to a stop at the base of a black gum tree. She only made one sharp yelp when he hit her—and then lay still where she stopped.

"Tiny!"

Frances started to rush toward her, but the first man grabbed her by the arm—mistake. She pivoted, crossed her leg in front of him, wrapped her other arm around his back and pulled. He rolled over her hip, landing on his back with a thud.

Her movement placed her between the downed man and the one that had hit Tiny. He reached forward to grab Frances—mistake number two.

She got a double handful of the front of his shirt, fell back toward the first man, brought her knee to her chest, put her foot in his stomach and shoved with all her might as she fell.

The second man sailed over her and landed on top of the first…

Me, Hutch, an' Mister Tom had carried the apples down into grandma's root seller where she kept all her vegetables like potatoes, carrots, onions, an' other things that needed to stay cool. There was also something 'bout 'em bein' below ground that kept 'em from spoilin'—don't understand it, but it does.

We went out the back door an' looked down the Red Hill Road.

"Wonder what's takin' Red so long? Shoulda been back by now."

From down the hill, we heard a faint yelp.

"That was Tiny! She's hurt...Somethin's wrong."

The three of us took off runnin' down Red Hill Road, listenin' for any more cries from her—nothin'...

Frances ran over, snatched up Tiny's limp form and sprinted back the way she'd come through the woods toward the road.

The two men untangled themselves, got to their feet, drew their Lugers, and gave chase.

The first man glanced at his friend as they ran. "Vhat happened?"

"I don't know. Von minute I vas grabbing for her, ze second I vas flying through ze air and landing on top of you."

THE POND

"Ve can't let her get avay."

"Nein."

Frances burst from the woods onto the road right in front of us. She had Tiny in her arms—she wasn't movin'.

"Two men, behind me!"

Mister Tom pulled the gun from his pocket.

"Down, everybody down."

We all hit the ground as two men in khaki's ran out from the woods where Fran did. Both carried guns. They stopped an' started shootin' at us.

Mister Tom held his Luger in both hands an' walked straight forward at those two fellas. They were shootin' all the time—but so was he.

Guess they didn't expect somebody to walk right at 'em while they were shootin' an' 'specially not shootin' back. Well, them fellas missed ever shot—but Mister Tom didn't.

Can see how come he got awarded the Medal of Honor in that war—he didn't know what fear was. Well, if he did, he ignored it. Then I remembered he told me one time, 'Without fear, there is no courage, Foot.' Gotta remember that.

Them two fellas both went sprawlin' on their faces in the red dirt like puppets with their strings cut. Mister Tom stopped right in front of 'em an' rolled each one over with his foot—nothin'. Dead as doornails.

We got to our feet.

Hutch looked at the two men an' shook his head. "Don't recognize either one. Ain't the same two as before."

I wasn't concerned with them right now, I was concerned with Tiny. Fran still held her close to her chest. Her little head was flopped over an' there was blood comin' from her ears an' nose.

The tears started to roll down my face like they were Fran's. I softly caressed Tiny's head.

"Tiny...my Tiny." I looked up, swallowed hard an' tried to breathe. "Had her since I was six, Red...She was just...just a...a puppy an' somebody...somebody had thrown her out...Tiny was my friend."

Hutch put his arm around my shoulders as they shook with my sobs...

§§§

CHAPTER SEVENTEEN

JAMISON HOME

"Do you need me to carry her?"

Fran shook her head. She was holdin' her lips tight—she couldn't talk.

Guess she was feelin' near bad as me on account Tiny was with her when it happened.

"Wadn't your fault, Red. It wadn't."

She just shook her head again. Tears were still runnin' down her face.

I looked up at the top of the hill, could see daddy an' mama had got to the house. They were headed downhill our way. Musta heard Mister Tom an' them fella's gunfire.

Mama came runnin' up an' saw Tiny's limp body in Fran's arms an' Hutch with his arm 'round my shoulders. I was still cryin', too.

"Oh, honey, I'm so sorry. Did she get shot?"

I shook my head. "One…one of the men…hit…hit her with a stick. She's gone, Mama…My Tiny's gone."

Hutch stepped back when mama reached out to hug me. She wrapped her arm around me an' I guess I just lost it. Got choked an' couldn't breathe for a minute. Reckon the gates kinda opened, best as I can remember.

Daddy walked 'long side mama an' next to Mister Tom as we headed back up the hill. "Was it those same Germans, Tom?"

Could see him shake his head. "Two different ones, Joe…but they both carried Lugers…picked 'em up." He pointed to 'em stuck in his belt. "Gotta go over to Jolley's Store and call the sheriff. Tell him to bring the meat wagon."

"Kill 'em both?"

"Yeah…They're layin' at the edge of the road back down the hill."

Daddy nodded. "Good."

I finally got my breath an' looked up. "I'm okay, Mama." I glanced over at Fran an' Tiny. "Gotta go dig a grave for her." I started cryin' again.

"We'll take care of it, honey."

I shook my head. "Uh-uh…She was my dog, Mama. I'm the one that has to do it."

Could see her glance over at daddy. She started cryin' too. He kinda smiled an' nodded. Their eyes were talkin', but I couldn't tell right off what they were sayin'.

We came in the yard, grandma an' grandpa were waitin' on the porch. She was twistin' a dish towel in her hands.

Grandma came down the steps to Fran. "Let me have her, honey, I'll wrap her in a baby blanket I have…I'm so sorry, Foot. We all loved her."

I just nodded. Couldn't talk no more. I turned around an' walked toward the barn to get one of grandpa's shovels. Hutch came with me.

Mister Tom an' daddy got in daddy's car—guess they were goin' to drive over to the store to use cousin Smead's phone.

I got a spade an' Hutch picked a sharpshooter.

"Think it'll be okay to bury her over under the Chinaberry tree at the side of the house. I want her close by."

He nodded. Knew wadn't nothin' he could say, but that's what friends are for.

I started diggin' a hole just her size. Got it shaped up an' Hutch took over with the sharpshooter to make it deeper, then I would clean it up.

In just a bit we almost had it deep enough. I didn't want any critters tryin' to dig down to her. I turned an' saw daddy an' Mister Tom drive back up. Guess they were done with the callin' an' the sheriff would be out pretty quick—'spect he was already on his way.

THE POND

I heard the front screen door slam, an' then Fran screamin' my name.

"Foot! Foot! Come quick!" She ran up to me an' Hutch.

I jabbed my shovel in the ground an' turned to her. "What is it?"

She grabbed my shoulders an' screamed in my face, tears were runnin' down her face again. "It's Tiny!...She's alive!...She's alive! Come on!"

"What?...Oh, my gosh."

I didn't bother with the steps to the porch, I just cleared them with one jump. Daddy an' Mister Tom were there fixin' to go in when Fran came runnin' out. Daddy opened the door for me.

Fran was right behind me. "Grandma's bedroom."

I wheeled to the left. Grandma an' mama had Tiny wrapped up warm on the bed with her head out an' kinda pillowed up. Mama had a damp rag she had cleaned the blood from her nose an' ears with.

Tiny was blinkin' an' looked up at me. When I reached my hand out, she gave it a weak lick. I started cryin' again, but these were happy tears.

Daddy an' Mister Tom came in the bedroom right behind me.

I sat on the edge of the bed an' gently stroked Tiny's head. There was a big knot in front of her left ear. Guess that's where that evil man hit her.

Mister Tom leaned over an' looked real close in each eye. He lifted her lip to look at her gums. They were pink.

He straightened up, turned to me and put his hand on my shoulder. "I believe she has a concussion, Foot." He shook his head. "No different than a human concussion...Need to keep her still for a few days, though. She doesn't need to do a lot of moving around...And keep her out of the sun...I think she's going to be all right."

I got up off the bed, hugged him, an' just nodded—I couldn't talk again.

Hutch leaned over to Fran. "What's a con-cussion?"

She leaned back. "I think it's when the brain kinda gets bruised when somebody gets hit on the head."

"Oh."

Grandma put her arm around my shoulders. "I'll make her a nice pallet in the corner of the spare bedroom across the hall where Ellie was…She doesn't need to be on the bed, she might try to get up and fall off. It's nice and dark in there."

I took a big breath. "I'll stay with her, make sure she don't get lonely an' think she's by herself."

"I'll stay too, Foot."

I nodded. "Thanks, Red."

"Me too."

I smiled at Hutch. Knew he would. "We can play cards or somethin' while we sit with her till she's better."

Everbody heard the front screen door slam. In a couple of seconds, the sheriff an' Doc Duckworth came in. Forgot the doctor would be comin'. He's also the county coroner or somethin' like that.

He moved over to the bed quickly, 'cause he could tell somethin' was wrong with Tiny.

"What happened?"

Fran took over on account she was there when it happened. "One of the men hit her with a limb. We thought she was dead, but she just started waking up."

"I'm pretty sure she has a concussion, Doc."

He glanced at Mister Tom, took a small flashlight from his bag, bent over, lifted first one eye lid, shined the light in her eye, then away. He did the same to the other one an' nodded.

"Good diagnosis, Tom." He took his stethoscope thing out an' listened to her chest. "Heart's strong and regular...Keep her warm and still."

"We're movin' her to that room where Ellie was. Grandma's puttin' a pallet on the floor...Gonna stay with her so she don't move around."

He nodded. "She should be a lot better in a couple of days, Foot. I'm not as familiar with canine trauma as with people, but it can't be all that different."

"That's what I thought, Doc. Saw a few concussed men in the war."

"I'm sure you did, Tom...You say there's two bodies down Red Hill Road?"

"That's correct." Mister Tom turned to the sheriff. "They came out of the woods chasin' Frances here. Started shooting at us." He shook his head. "Couldn't allow that."

THE POND

"He walked right straight at 'em, Sheriff…firin' that Luger of his, them shootin' at 'im all the while. They missed…Mister Tom didn't. Shot 'em down like mad dogs."

The sheriff looked at me, then at Mister Tom—his eyes real big. "You don't say?"

"Not much difference, far as I was concerned…Just glad Foot, Hutch, and I got down there when we did."

The sheriff nodded. "Just heard Pete and Charlie pull up with the ambulance. Guess we need to show them where the bodies are."

Fran stepped forward. "I'll go too. I can show you where they first came up while I was pickin' berries for grandma…Need to get the bucket of berries I had already picked, anyway."

Grandma put her hand on Fran's shoulder. "Oh, honey, don't worry about those berries."

"I've got to bring your bucket back to you, it just happens to be almost full of dewberries."

Grandma opened her mouth to say somethin' but guess thought better of it. Knew Fran was goin' to go anyway.

Fran had a big grin on her face when she turned to me an' Hutch. "Besides, I can show where I threw both of those men to the ground using that judo stuff, ya'll showed me...It was how I was able to get away with Tiny."

Mister Tom's mouth dropped open. "You threw both of those men? My stars, they're bigger than I am."

Joe shook his head and hugged Fran. "Your mama used to do the same thing to me when I was your age, but she was two years older than I was."

She nodded, still grinnin'. "They tried to grab me an' we'd been practicing judo on that very thing. I hip-tossed the first one to his back, then the other reached for me an' I did the back throw thing an' he landed on top of the first man...I picked Tiny up an' ran like crazy."

The sheriff shook his head, smiled, an' looked at everbody else in the room. "Sounds like we have two heroes here...Amazing, simply amazing. Thought I'd heard it all."

SPRING MOTEL - EL DORADO

Amell set his warm bottle of Becks beer on the table against the wall and looked at Elias, Jonas, and the remaining member of his team, Bernard Braun. "Maynard and Andreas should have been back by now mit one of zose kids."

Jonas took a swig of his beer. "Told you zhey are ver resourceful children...Vhat zhey did to Elias and me."

Amell glared at Jonas. "Maynard and Andreas are trained assassins...Zhey von't be bested by mere children."

Jonas shrugged and had another sip. "As you zay."

Elias leaned back against the headboard of one of the beds. "Zo...now vhat?"

Amell turned his glare to Elias. "Ve do vhat ve have to do. Ve must find ze Gypsy Jew...Ze Reich does not tolerate failure."

§§§

CHAPTER EIGHTEEN

RED HILL ROAD

Sheriff Wilson led the way in his black county Ford with Doctor Duckworth, Tom, and Frances as passengers. There was a gold five pointed star on the front doors with County Sheriff - Union County underneath. The county coroner's ambulance was behind him.

THE POND

He stopped as Tom pointed to the bodies just off the road in the small bushes and tall grass. The ambulance pulled up behind him. Pete and Charlie got out, walked to the back to open the doors, and got a stretcher.

Tom, the sheriff, and Doctor Duckworth stepped up to the bodies.

Both were face up, the way Tom left them. Sheriff Wilson leaned over with his hands on his knees and looked at the bullet wounds.

"Great guns, Tom. Two shots to the center of the chest of each man...I can't put my finger between 'em. That's some kind of shooting, especially while being shot at."

He went through both men's pockets and held up a set of car keys.

"Any identification, Myron?"

He looked back at the doctor as he raised up. "Nothin', Ralph...Just these keys."

Tom handed the sheriff the two Lugers he had picked up. "Here are their weapons."

Sheriff Wilson popped the magazine from one and shook his head. He looked at Tom.

"This hold eight rounds?"

He nodded. "Plus one in the chamber."

The sheriff counted the remaining rounds in each box. "One has two rounds left the other just one." He glanced back up at Tom. "You faced either thirteen or fifteen rounds semiautomatic fire at less than thirty feet?"

Tom shrugged. "Target shooting is a lot different than combat shooting, Sheriff...I'm guessing these men had not had a lot of close combat exchanges in their background...They were panic shooting...I wasn't."

Both the doctor and the sheriff just looked at Tom in awe and admiration.

Doctor Duckworth knelt down to double check if the men had any pulse. "Know this isn't necessary, but it's protocol. Death looks as if it were almost instantaneous...Both rounds to the heart." He turned and nodded to the attendants.

"They're all yours, gentlemen."

Pete and Charlie, both veterans of WWII as Army medics, approached. Each held out their hands to Tom.

"Just want to shake the hand of an honest to God Medal of Honor recipient...It's a rare privilege, Gunnery Sergeant Rayford...a rare privilege. Been wantin' to meet you." Pete shook Tom's hand.

Charlie did the same. Then both Army veterans stepped back, snapped to attention, and saluted him as is traditional for any military person, enlisted or officer, when meeting a Congressional Medal of Honor recipient.

Tom returned the salute, looking a little embarrassed. "Thank you, gentlemen."

Pete and Charlie picked up the litter they brought from the truck, loaded the first body on it, grinned and nodded at each other, and headed to the back of the ambulance.

They returned to get the second body with another stretcher.

"Want to show us where this started, young lady?"

"Yessir, this way."

Fran led the way into the woods along the narrow game trail. The large cluster of dewberry vines were in a small open area almost fifty yards into the dense forest of mostly pines. There were also a few scattered hickory, pecan, and gum trees.

She stopped at the area of vines and picked up her bucket—almost full of ripe dewberries.

"The two men came at me from that way." She pointed down toward the meadow. "There's the tree they knocked Tiny over to...an' right here is where I threw the first man down...an' there, between him an' where Tiny was layin', is where I fell to my back an' flipped the other man over on top of him. That gave me time to pick her up an' run like a crazy person back to the road...Ya'll know the rest."

Tom patted her shoulder. "That was some cool-headed thinkin', Fran...Real proud of you."

She shrugged her shoulders a little. "Well, that's the thing, Mister Tom, I don't remember think..."

"I know, hon, that's the way it always happens. There's no time to think, you just react and do what you have to."

"Any idea where they could have come from, Tom?"

"Well, given the road dead ends about a mile further on, I would guess that since they didn't drive by the house...they most likely parked at a old loggin' road about a quarter mile that way." He pointed to the east.

THE POND

"Do you know how to get there from the Haynesville Road?"

"I do."

"Well, let's head up to Big John's, shall we."

The ambulance had already left by the time they got to the road.

They loaded up in the sheriff's car, drove down to the meadow to turn around, and headed to the house to drop Frances off.

"Tell John an' Mame where we've gone an' we'll be back in a bit...Hate to miss Mame's supper."

"Yessir." Frances grinned, got out from the rear seat and carried the bucket toward the house as the sheriff drove off.

They drove southeast almost a mile to an old, grass in the middle, logging road. The sheriff turned in, and a half-mile down the rutted lane, came to a parked Chevrolet sedan.

The sheriff opened the driver's door with his handkerchief and looked inside. "Bet a dollar this is a rent car." He looked over the top of the vehicle at Tom on the other side. "Check the glove box, Tom. Use your handkerchief...you don't mind."

"Right." He opened the door, reached in and pressed the button to the glove compartment, and removed a folder of papers after the cover fell forward. "Says National Car Rental - Dallas, Texas, Sheriff." Tom handed him the folder over the top.

The sheriff removed the first document, the rental agreement, and read the name beside the signature. "Amell Schmidt."

Doctor Duckworth shook his head. "Well, don't believe that fellow is Irish."

"Nope, definitely German, but we don't know which one he was." The sheriff looked up from the document and raised his eyebrows. "If either."

"Or neither...as I recall those other two were a Jonas and an Elias...Say where he's from?"

Sheriff Wilson flipped through the documents, frowned, and looked back at Tom. "Well, well, this is interesting. Gives his home address as in Posadas, Misiones Province...Argentina."

Tom shook his head. "Not a bit surprised, Sheriff. I didn't think those two men earlier were from the Fatherland."

"How so?"

"Their accents were muted somewhat...I was guessing, South America...Argentina, Paraguay, or Bolivia...Spanish is the predominant language."

The doctor looked puzzled. "Where is this Posadas town?"

Tom turned to him. "Far northern Argentina...close to the border with Paraguay."

"That's where a lot of the Nazi officials fled to at the end of WWII, isn't it?"

Tom nodded again. "What they say...including the rumors that Hitler faked his suicide and went there by submarine."

The sheriff turned and headed to his vehicle. "Need to radio for a tow truck. Have this hauled in to the county lot and get a deputy to dust it for prints, then give it a good goin' over...Let's go...I've got the keys in my pocket."

He got the vehicle turned around and headed to the Haynesville Road.

Once they turned back northwest, he picked up the mic from the clip on the dash and radioed his office. "Mabel, this is the sheriff. - Over."

"What's going on, Sheriff? - Over."

"Call county and have them send a tow truck to a small loggin' road a half-mile southeast of

Jolley's Store on the Haynesville Road…west side. - Over."

"Ten-four, Sheriff. - Over."

"Have 'em take it to the county lot and tell Mervin to dust it and give it a good look-see for anything unusual. - Over."

"Roger that. Anything else? - Over."

"Negative. Sheriff out." He hung the mic back on the clip above the radio.

"Handy as handles on a jug." The sheriff glanced over at his long time friend, Doctor Duckworth, sitting in the passenger seat.

"Yep, saves a lot of time."

He pulled up in front of John's house, next to Joe's pale green Ford and stopped.

The three men walked up the flagstone path to the porch where John and Joe were sitting in calf hide bottomed rockers.

"How's Tiny?"

Joe smiled. "She's better, Tom. Completely awake now, but Foot, Frances, and Hutch are still sitting with her…Ya'll find the car?"

"Good…and yes we did."

"Rent car from Dallas."

John looked at the sheriff and frowned. "Dallas?…To those two Germans?"

"Yes and no."

"Don't play games, Myron."

He grinned. "Yes, from Dallas, John, and no, not those two Germans…a third one and with an address in Argentina…The two Tom shot were not the same."

"Come again…Think I'm gettin' confused."

"Fact is we don't know how many men there may be…at least three, maybe four more, I'd say. I'm convinced they're *all* Germans and from Argentina."

Joe and John both looked at Tom. Finally Joe nodded.

"Ah, that's where they think all those Nazis escaped to…includin' Eichmann and Mengele, isn't it?"

Tom nodded. "It is…among others. The nucleus of a reinvigorated Third or a Fourth Reich."

The doctor raised an eyebrow. "Mengele, the Doctor of Death."

"Tom frowned. "Yeah, him."

Joe pressed his lips together and his jaw muscles rippled. "So we may not be done with the Nazis yet?"

Tom nodded. "Kind of smells that way, Joe."

§§§

CHAPTER NINETEEN

SPRING MOTEL - EL DORADO

"Verdammt!" Amell threw his empty bottle of Becks against the wall, shattering it and scattering glass in a wide area around the room. "Zhey are either dead or arrested or zhey vould be here."

"I zink ve zhould leave zhis place."

Amell glared at Jonas. "Zhen vhat do you zuggest?"

"Ve should go zomevhere else...quickly."

Amell nodded. "*Ja*...Agree. Vether zhey vere killed or captured, ze authorities vill eventually find ze automobile. Ze paperwork for ze rental has my name on zhem."

Bernard frowned. "Vhere do ve go? Ze sheriff vill check motels in ze county."

Jonas glanced at Elias. "Didn't ve see a motel in Haynesville?"

"*Ja*, ve did."

"But, zhey vill check all ze motels."

Elias grinned and shook his head. "Amell, Haynesville iz not only not in zhis county...It iz not in zhis ztate. It iz in vhat zhey call Louisiana...Originally settled by ze French."

Jonas grinned. "And ve know about ze French."

Amell's eyes brightened as his head bobbed. "Ah...*Ja*, iz goot."

JAMISON HOME

"Mame, these are the best pork chops I've ever had."

"Oh, Myron, fiddlesticks. You say that about everything I fix."

"Only because it's true, Mame, only because it's true."

"Everything is so good and goes perfect with your pork chops...the speckled butter beans, fried okra, fried squash, fresh sliced tomatoes, buttermilk cornbread, and the pickled cucumbers and onions."

Mister Tom wiped his mouth. "Wait till you wrap your tongue around a spoonful of her dewberry cobbler, Doc."

"Oh, my, yes. Been smelling that since we got here."

Me, Hutch, an' Fran looked at each other an' we all nodded. We been smellin' that cobbler too—thanks to Frances Ann.

Grandpa set his half empty second mug of clabber back on the table an' wiped the white mustache from his lip. "Get your radioin' done, Myron?"

He nodded. "I did. Told Mabel I wanted every available deputy searching the area motels for those Germans...and to call the Chief at the El Dorado PD to get his men on it in town, too...They been here for a while, gotta be staying somewhere."

I felt somethin' by my leg. I looked down an' there sat Tiny, lookin' up at me with those big brown eyes.

"Well, you're feelin' good enough you want some of grandma's pork chops, don't you?"

"Go ahead and cut one up in little chunks, Foot. She deserves it."

I glanced up at the opposite end of the table from grandpa where grandma's place was. "Yessum."

Got another one from the platter, started cuttin' it into little square pieces an' feedin' 'em to her one at the time. She musta been really hungry 'cause she was scarfin' 'em down.

"One is probably enough, Foot...don't want to give her too much. Sometimes concussions are accompanied by nausea."

"Yessir, Doctor Duckworth."

Hutch leaned over to Fran. "What's nausea?"

"Sick to your stomach."

"Ah...Had that a time or two."

"Wouldn't hurt to take her outside to do her business, hon...when she's done. She probably needs to go by now."

"Okay, Mama."

THE POND

She finished that pork chop jam-up quick an' I got up from the bench. All us kids sat on 'long one side of the table—grownups got chairs.

Fran an' Hutch got up, too.

"We'll go with you, cuz."

I looked back at her as I picked Tiny up. "Ya'll come on, then."

We went out in the front yard an' I set her down on the ground. Sure 'nuff, she didn't waste no time in doin' her thing.

"Wow, she was really holdin' it, wasn't she?"

I turned back to Fran to reply an' caught somethin' out of the corner of my eye over to the barn. "Looks like Unka Dud is here again. Watch Tiny for a minute, Red, be right back."

I looked behind the house toward the Haynesville Road, both ways, then ran up the steps an' inside.

When I got to the dinin' room where everbody still was, I stepped up to the end of the table.

"Grandma, can you fix a plate...Unka Dud is over in the shadow of the barn watchin' us like he was when we tasted the watermelons. Know he's most likely hungry."

"Any sign of that black Ford, Foot?"

"No, sir, Mister Tom. I looked real close over to the road...both ways."

"Then go back outside and bring the poor man in here. I'll fix him a proper plate." Grandma got to her feet.

"Yes, ma'am." I turned an' hustled out the door an' down the dog run to outside.

I picked Tiny up an' headed to the gate.

"Where you goin'?"

I looked back at Hutch. "To get Unka Dud. Grandma's fixin' him a plate."

He an' Fran joined me.

"Is it safe?"

I glanced at Fran. "Believe so."

Could tell he saw us comin'. Knew it wouldn't bother him none 'cause we'd brought him those slices of watermelon when he was here before.

He glanced at Tiny in my arms as we walked up to him in the shadows. "Iz your dog hurt, son?"

I nodded. "One of them German men knocked her out earlier, but she's better...Grandma says for you to come in the house, she's fixin' you a plate...It don't do to argue with grandma."

He smiled. "No, I've met Mame. Vonderful lady...I'm assuming those men aren't around?"

"Nope. Checked real good 'fore I went inside. Mister Tom's done killed two of 'em today down Red Hill Road a ways."

"Really?"

"Uh-huh. They were tryin' to kidnap Red, here…that's when they hit Tiny with a club an' knocked her out…Guess they thought they could make us tell where you were…Didn't work."

"Oh, my…I'm zorry."

"Tiny's lots better now."

We got him inside the house quick as we could, anyway.

"There's the warsh stand there at the end of the hall. Best clean up first…"

"I know. Mame requires clean hands."

I nodded.

Soon as he dried his hands, we went into the dinin' room. Grandma pointed to an empty chair at the table between Mister Tom an' daddy.

"Sit there, Eric."

She had really filled his plate. I could tell by his eyes he was hungry when he sat down.

He looked up at grandma. "Thank you, Mame. You didn't have to do zhis."

"Well, didn't think you'd eaten."

"No, madam."

He spread his napkin in his lap, lowered his head an' closed his eyes. Guess he was sayin' a silent blessin'.

The sheriff, Mister Tom, an' grandpa didn't bother him till he was done eatin'—'cludin' a big bowl of cobbler.

"I assume you know there's some Germans looking for you, Mister Hoffer...or is it Bieler?"

He looked up, kinda surprised, at Sheriff Wilson. He set down the cup of coffee grandma had put in front of him when she removed his plate an' bowl.

"I zee zhey know who I am, zhen."

"Apparently so. I think their organization has been looking for you a long time...They think we know where you are."

Unka Dud, or Mister Bieler, nodded. "The *Freikorps*. Zhey are now ze vile Nazis."

Mister Tom turned to him. "Do you know why?"

"*Ja.*" He looked around the table. "I am a Jew...A Gypsy Jew. Ve are converted Jewish

Christians…a very small sect. Ve vere entrusted mit certain valuable items and treasure vhen ze *Freikorps* started rising to power because of ze vay ve can move around."

"Before the war?"

He glanced at Mister Tom. "*Ja*, before ze zo-called var to end all vars…Zhose of us mit ze treasures scatted around ze vorld…I came to America."

"What is it you brought here that's so valuable?"

Unka Dud looked down at the end of the table at grandpa. "I'd rather not zay, John. It's zafer zat vay…for everyone."

"What about those two skeletons from your pond?"

He looked at the coffee in his cup for a minute or so, then at the sheriff. "Ze vere my brothers."

Unka Dud leaned back an' took a breath. I think everbody else forgot to breathe, then.

"Three of ze *Freikorps* found us right after ze var started. Zhey tortured my brothers, zhen executed zhem, vhen zhey vouldn't talk." He nodded an' I could hear him grit his teeth. "I found zem, but too late…Ze murderers paid."

211

"You killed them?"

His dark eyes suddenly took on a real cold look when he stared off into space, not really seein' nothin'. "Yes…I burned ze bodies…Zhey didn't deserve to be buried."

"There on your place?"

He nodded at the sheriff.

"Ze wild hogs took care of any bones left…I vas in hopes zhey couldn't find me again…I guess I vas wrong."

Mister Tom patted him on the shoulder. "Well, they haven't found you, yet."

He nodded. "Zhey are very persistent to get vhat I have."

"Are you armed?"

Unka Dud glanced around the table an' nodded, an' then looked at Sheriff Wilson. "Am I in trouble for killing zhose Germans?"

The sheriff kinda arched one eyebrow. "What Germans…Eric? We have a law here in the United States about *Corpus Delicti*."

Unka Dud nodded. "No body, no crime."

"Pretty much."

Glad Unka Dud knew what it was, 'cause I didn't have no idea.

THE POND

THERIOT'S MOTEL - HAYNESVILLE, LA.

Jonas, Elias, Amell, and Bernard checked into two side by side rooms in a U shaped single story motel. The standard configuration for most motels across the country.

Their single vehicle, the black Ford sedan was parked in front of the rooms.

The four met in Amell and Bernard's room.

"Vat if Andreas and Maynard are not dead or arrested?"

Amell looked at Bernard with a degree of disdain and shook his head. "Like I zaid, I zink zhey are dead…Zhey vould never zurrender."

Jonas shook his head. "No, zhey vould not. But, zhere are still four of us. Ve vill find zhat *verflucht Zigeuner Jude*." He glanced at his partner. "Elias and I have determined he lives mitin valking distance from zhat Big John's place."

Amell nodded. "Ve begin zhere…Everyone check your veapons…Zen ve go eat."

§§§

CHAPTER TWENTY

JAMISON HOME

"My brothers and I got here in 1915 mit vhat we had to bring from Europe…I bought zhat land zhat adjoins John and ve built ze log cabin and a place to hide ze things ve brought in a little over four months.

"Zhere vas plenty of trees available and ve vere all trained carpenters and built houses back home.

THE POND

My brothers vent to town to get supplies one day and didn't come back..."

"That when the *Freikorps* found you?"

"*Ja*, Tom...Except zhey found my brothers in town. Zhey didn't know vhere ve had built."

Grandpa shook his head. "How, then, did you track down your brothers?"

"Ve had been fighting ze *Freikorps* for two years already...I knew how zhey zhought."

"But how in the world did you find them?"

Unka Dud studied the cup in his hand for a minute before lookin' up at daddy. "It took me four days to run zhem down to an abandoned farm house south of Jolley's Chapel Cemetery..."

Grandpa nodded. "Know where you're talking about. Burned down in early 1916...Was that you?"

"*Ja*...After ze fight." He looked at grandma an' mama. "You'll pardon me ladies."

"You just go on with your story, Eric, don't mind us or the kids...not after what they've already been through."

"Zank you, Mame...I found ze house because ze *dummkopfs* left ze Ford truck of ours zhat my brothers had driven to town parked outside...Ve had two."

"Was it day time or night?"

"Night, Tom...I slipped up to a vindow vhere zhere vas a light from a couple of lanterns inside. I peeked in and saw my brothers tied in chairs..." He stopped an' stared for a minute 'cross the pasture to the south. "...I knew immediately zhey vere both dead. Could see ze bullet holes in zhere foreheads...*Freikorps* execution style...and ze blood zhat soaked zhere bodies. Ze fiends had removed zheir shirts zo zhey could burn zhem mit hot irons and cigarettes...My brothers vould never talk."

He glanced over where the sun was settlin' down close to the tops of the trees to the west an' blinked several times.

"You don't have to tell us the rest, Eric."

Unka Dud turned to grandma. "It's all right, Mame, I've never been able to talk to anyone about zhis before...I need to. It's time."

She nodded. "I understand...Go ahead then, get it all out."

Grandma was good at recognizin' how people felt inside.

"Zank you…" He took a breath. "I could also see bruises on zheir faces…Didn't know until later about ze broken fingers and other bones."

"You say there were three of them?"

"*Ja*, Joe, three…just standing next to my brothers, smoking cigarettes…One vas still holding a Mauser C96 in his hand…Zink he had shot zhem just before I got zhere. I could see veapons in holsters on ze other two. I couldn't tell vhat type…Later I found zhey vere also Mausers."

"So, you just burst into the room…one against three?"

Unka Dud glanced at grandpa an' nodded. "*Ja*, John, me, and surprise…Zhat's two to three. I felt zhose vere goot odds."

Mister Tom also nodded. "I could agree with that. Surprise can even a lot of odds…Like when Sam Houston's army of around 900 defeated General Santa Anna's Mexican force of over 1400 at San Jacinto to end Texas' battle for independence in 1836…He was outnumbered almost two to one and only lost eleven men to Santa Anna's 650 killed. The battle lasted some eighteen minutes…You sound like you had some training, Eric."

"*Ja*...I am a member of ze counter Aryan or counter *Friedkops* underground. Ve all had commando and assassin training...Georg Luger vas a personal friend and he had given me one of ze new Luger PO8s.

"I eased to ze front door and slipped inside. Could hear zhem talking about vhat to do next. How to find me...Zhat's vhen I didn't give zhem ze chance...Ze door to ze hallvay vas open. I stepped in...'Here I am, *vipern.*'"

Mister Tom had kind of a grin. "You shot the man holding the Mauser in his hand first?"

He glanced over at him an' nodded. "*Ja*...he vas first, zhen I moved to ze left, firing zhat Luger at ze other two...Didn't take long. Zhey fell almost on top of each other...It vas such a surprise, zhey never got zheir guns out of ze holsters."

"Is your Luger a .9mm or a 7.65?"

"It iz an early P08...7.65 Parabellum."

Hutch leaned over close to me. "What's para-bellum?"

I shook my head. "No idea." Wadn't gonna interrupt to ask. Find out later.

"Asked Jesus to bless my brothers as best I could. I crossed myself and zhem, and zhen carried zhem one at a time out to ze truck…I came back and got ze three *Friedkops*."

Sheriff Wilson shook his head. "If you hauled the killers off, why did you burn that old house?"

"Blood, Sheriff…Zhat room vas soaked in blood…from both my brothers and zheir killers. I didn't vant ze authorities looking for ze causes."

The sheriff nodded. "That makes sense. All that blood would have certainly created a stir."

"I drove back over to our cabin, unloaded ze vermin vhere ve had piled our scrap vood from building ze cabin, stacked more branches and limbs on top…and burned it."

"What about your brothers?"

He glanced at grandpa. "I wrapped zhem in canvas, veighted each down mit some rocks, and carried zhem on my back over to ze pond…My brothers vere both sailors. Couldn't bury zhem at sea like zhey vould vant, so I chose ze pond…You know ze rest."

Mister Tom nodded. "And over the years, the canvas and rope rotted away. Lot can happen in thirty-four years."

Unka Dud sorta grimaced. "And now it starts again."

Mister Tom glanced at the sheriff, grandpa an' daddy. "Except now…you're not alone."

He nodded. "Zank you."

Unka Dud got to his feet from the rocker he was sittin' in out on the porch.

"Vell, I suppose I should get started home."

Him an' all the other grownups had been out there havin' after dinner coffee when the stories got 'round to his.

Me, Hutch, an' Fran were sittin' on the edge of the porch—Tiny was in her lap. We were listenin' to Mister Tom's stories, an' then Unka Dud's.

The sheriff an' Doctor Duckworth got up 'cause they had to go home, too—up north to El Dorado.

Grandma turned to Unka Dud. "I better get you a lantern, Eric. It'll be dark before you get there through the woods."

"May have a point zhere, Mame…zank you."

She went inside, an' then came out carryin' a coal oil lamp with a wire bail an' a metal base instead of a glass one, an' handed it to him. It was already lit.

"Just turn the wick up as you need to." She handed him a gallon jug of buttermilk with a wire handle. "Here, had some extra buttermilk."

"Yes, madam, zank you…I'll get zhis lamp and jug back to you."

"Take your time…Be careful."

Unka Dud nodded an' lifted his other hand in a wave as he walked to the gate.

I could see the bulge in the back pocket of his khakis, an' since he said he was armed, figured that was it.

He disappeared down across the pasture toward the woods in the twilight. The lamp was just a spot of light hangin' from his right hand as he got close to the fence of grandpa's property line.

I nudged Hutch in the ribs. "Now you can ask your question."

"Uh, Mister Tom?"

"What is it, Hutch?"

"What's that word para-bellum that Unka Dud used mean?"

"Well, parabellum is actually Latin and it means, 'prepare for war'. A Parabellum weapon or bullet is basically for wartime."

Hutch nodded. "So that Luger of yours an' Mister Joe's .45 are para-bellum?"

"Correct."

He turned to me. "How's come you didn't know that?"

I shrugged my shoulders. "I heard it the same time you did...jaybird."

Tiny got up from Fran's lap an' looked off toward the woods on the other side of grandpa's truck patch. The hair stood up on her back an' a low growl rumbled in her throat.

"What is it, honey?" Fran stroked her.

It was gettin' too dark to see by now since the sun set while Unka Dud was walkin' cross the pasture headin' home.

"Somethin' over yonder she don't like."

Hutch glanced over at me. "Or somebody."

Jonas pulled the field glasses down from his eyes and looked over at Amell as the four stood just inside the woods. "Zat vas Bieler, valking across ze pasture and disappearing into ze voods...I'm sure of it. He vas carrying a lantern."

THE POND

"Do you zink he vas going to his house? You zaid you and Elias thought he lived mitin valking distance."

"*Ja.*"

§§§

CHAPTER TWENTY-ONE

JAMISON HOME

"Ya'll keep your eyes and ears open, now." The sheriff looked back at grandpa, Mister Tom, an' daddy as him an' the doctor went down the steps.

Grandpa nodded. "Yep, that's our intention, Myron...Stayin' armed, too."

"Need a ride over to your place, Tom?"

THE POND

"Oh, think not, Sheriff. Believe I'll walk…Enjoy the evening."

"Do you need a lantern, Tom?"

He turned. "Not really, Mame. Know the way blindfolded…Moon'll be coming up soon. Thanks anyway."

WOODS

"Ve better leave in case ze sheriff sees our vehicle parked back up at zee road." Jonas turned and led the others back toward the Haynesville Road.

Amell was directly behind him. "Now zat ve know ze direction Bieler vas valkink, tomorrow ve shall find a vay to zee vhere he vas goink."

"Ja." Elias nodded. "I zink he vould head in a fairly straight line to go home."

JAMISON HOME

Mister Tom, the sheriff, an' Doctor Duckworth all left at the same time.

Tiny watched the woods 'cross the road for a few more minutes, then she turned away an' laid back down with her head in Fran's lap.

Daddy looked at her, then across the road. "Could be a wolf, coyote, or bobcat…But, if that was those Germans over there, they must have left when the sheriff and Tom did."

"You think they could have seen where Unka Dud went, Daddy?"

He nodded. "Most likely, Hoss Fly…If they were watching, they couldn't help but see which way he went."

Grandma got back up. "I'll go fix ya'll's pallets. You getting just about ready for bed?"

"Yessum, been kind of a long day." I glanced at Hutch an' Fran, they nodded.

She smiled. "Thought you might say that."

Daddy an' mama also got to their feet.

"We best head to the house too. I'm still on daylights…Be up early. My turn to drive."

Mama an' daddy gave us good night hugs an' headed out down the walk to get in the car.

I took Tiny out into the yard so she could do her business 'fore we hit the sack. She piddled around for a minute or so, sniffin' stuff, before she finally went.

By the time we got back inside, grandma had our pallets ready, so we washed up, brushed our teeth, an' crawled under the quilt—that was all we needed on account it hadn't started coolin' off much yet. Tiny laid between me an' Fran as we watched the half moon peekin' above the tree line as it rose.

I locked my hands behind my head while I studied the sky. "Believe we need to go tell Unka Dud 'bout him may have been watched walk toward home, tomorra after breakfast."

Hutch rolled over an' propped up on one elbow. "Are you crazy?...No, don't answer that, already know."

Fran turned toward me, I could see her blue eyes twinkle in the new moonlight.

"Knew it was too good to last."

I looked over at her. "What?"

"Been here for three days and haven't gotten in big trouble yet."

"Three days? Gotta be some kinda record for Foot."

I elbowed Hutch in the ribs. "Well, ya'll don't have to come along, you know."

"Huh…Who's gonna bail your sorry butt out when you step in it?"

I could hear Fran mumble as she dropped off to sleep.

"Yeah, who?"

All three of us sat bolt upright 'bout thirty minutes 'fore dawn when Rosco welcomed the comin' day right outside the door. Guess we'd been pretty tired 'cause we were sleepin' hard.

Could hear him fluff his wings 'fore he let loose again.

Hutch shook his head. "Sha-zam! No sleepin' in with that big boy right outside."

I lent Hutch some of my Captain Marvel comic books—think he found a new word he likes. I know I tried that magic word a couple times—didn't work for me neither.

Fran rubbed the sleep from her eyes with her knuckles, an' then blinked several times. "Wow, didn't know I was so tired."

THE POND

I looked down between us an' Tiny hadn't stirred, guess she was still recouperatin'.

Could hear grandma already in the kitchen gettin' her fire started an' puttin' the coffee on. The screen door at the front slammed as grandpa headed out to the barn to milk Sally an' feed Ted—the day was started.

We trundled into the kitchen after makin' our trip to the outhouse. Could smell the bacon sizzlin' when we came in the back screen door.

Grandma was stirrin' up some scrambled eggs to go with the bacon an' the biscuits she just took out of the oven—she makes best biscuits in the whole world. I usually stuck a couple in my bib pockets for later.

"What do you ruffians have planned for today?"

I glanced at Fran an' Hutch. "Oh, not much, reckon we'll do some bird huntin' with our sling shots, Grandma."

I handed Tiny a piece of bacon under the table. Knew she was waitin' on one. Then I gave her the rinds grandma had cut off an' fried up crisp for her—she loves 'em.

"Well, ya'll stay away from the pond, hear?"

We turned as grandpa came in the door with a near full milk bucket—he set it on the counter for grandma to strain.

"Yessir."

Hutch an' Fran looked over at me. Both of 'em had their eyebrows lifted up.

We finished our breakfast all 'bout the same time.

"Tiny, you stay here, today…Can we be excused, Grandma?"

"Of course, I'll fix Tiny a pad by the stove, she likes it in here with me…Ya'll stay out of trouble, now."

"Yessum."

Don't know why everbody always says that.

We got up an' headed down the dog run to the front door an' outside—we'd made sure we had plenty of marbles in our pockets 'fore we sat down at the table.

"What are we gonna do, now? Mister John said to stay away from the pond."

I grinned as I glanced over at Hutch. "He didn't say which pond…did he?"

THE POND

He puffed his cheeks an' blew his breath out. "Lordy, Lordy."

Fran shook her head. "Oboy…here we go."

We went through the gate by the barn an' headed toward the woods to the south. Gave grandpa's pond a wide berth, 'case he was watchin'. Even though there was a nice size grove of wild plums behind the dam, we'd done had breakfast anyways.

Ate a bunch of 'em last year while they were still a bit green—think I threw up my toenails. Learned a lesson there—don't eat wild plums 'fore they're ripe.

We crawled through the four wire fence at grandpa's back property line an' into Unka Dud's property. I put my foot on the third wire an' lifted the second one up for Fran an' Hutch, then he did the same so I could climb through without snaggin' my overalls on a barb.

There was a kind of trail us an' my cousins, Don an' Hubert had made over the years to Unka Dud's pond.

The woods were pretty thick 'tween the fence an' the pond. Lots of pine with some hickory, pecan, an' couple different kinds of oak—not countin' the dewberry an' whoa vines.

We got out our sling shots out an' were pickin' up some hickory nuts an' burr oak acorns as we walked.

The woods was full of all kinds an' manner of birds singin' their songs an' flittin' from tree to tree—an' squirrels gatherin' nuts, too. They were fussin' at us probably 'cause we were pickin' up what they considered their winter food source.

We were gettin' close to Unka Dud's pond, could see it shinin' through the trees. I stopped, loaded up a hickory nut, an' let fly at a fox squirrel barkin' at me from a pecan limb 'bout fifteen feet above the ground. He scooted along the limb back toward the trunk when I fired.

My hickory nut bounced off the limb right where he had been. He stopped when he got to the trunk, ran around to the other side, then peeked back at us an' gave us what for. Was probably sayin', *'Naya, naya...missed me,'* in squirrel.

Fran loaded up a burr oak acorn after she popped the cap off it, pulled the rubbers back an' let fly at 'im. That big ol' acorn ricocheted off the trunk, shatterin' some of the shell off, an' makin'

THE POND

Mister Squirrel duck back behind where we couldn't see 'im—he'll probably appreciate that acorn when he picks it up.

"Pretty good shot there, Red...You been practicin'."

She shook her head, swingin' her flamin' red pony tail from side to side. "Not really...I'm just a natural."

Both me an' Hutch bent over like we were throwin' up an' gaggin'.

"Shhhh."

We raised back up an' noticed she had her hand up in the air, shushin' us.

I looked at Hutch, then at her. "What?"

"Notice all the critters went silent?"

I cocked my head—it was quiet as a mouse peein' on a cotton ball.

I glanced back at Fran, then at Hutch. "Somebody's in these woods that don't belong."

§§§

CHAPTER TWENTY-TWO

JAMISON HOME

"Anybody home?" Tom knocked on the back screen door.

"Come on in, Tom."

He came through the spring-loaded door and into the kitchen, being careful not to let it slam shut. "Mornin', Mame."

THE POND

"Morning, Tom. Coffee?"

"Yessum, you don't mind?"

"You know better…You're welcome in our house anytime. Sit yourself down." She set a white ceramic mug on the breakfast table and filled it with coffee—aware that he always took it black.

He had a sip. "Mmm, always great coffee, Mame."

"Thank you, had breakfast?"

"Yessum, I'm good…Where's John?"

"He's down in the bottom field plowing under the pea vines since we've already harvested."

"The kids?"

"Said they were going bird hunting with their sling shots."

"Know which way they went?"

She was cutting some salt pork to put in the greens that would be ready by dinnertime. "Didn't watch…John just told them to stay away from the pond."

Tom turned his head and stared out the screen door as he absentmindedly picked up his cup and had another sip.

THE POND

"Now vhere do ve go?" Amell looked around the bank of the pond. "Ze trail led directly to zis lake."

Elias pointed to the water. "Look at zhat…it's like glass. Reminds me of lakes in ze Black Forest back in ze Fatherland zhat are zaid to be haunted."

Jonas glared at him. "*Du bist bescheuert.*"

"Zhere is nothing 'stupid' about it. Zhat is vhat it looks like."

Amell pointed to his right. "Shut up…Ve go around zhis vay and keep goink in ze zame direction."

He turned to lead the three other men the way he indicated when he was hit on the shoulder by something hard.

"*Ach du lieber Gott!…Vas ist das?*" He grabbed his shoulder where he was hit and looked at the ground where a hickory nut was still bouncing away.

We hunkered down behind a bush when the man I'd hit glanced our direction after lookin' up in the trees.

THE POND

I leaned my head over close to my cousin's. "Stay close 'tween me an' Hutch, Red. We know these woods like grandma's back yard...Gonna get these yahoos lost." I pointed at the man next to the one I hit. "Pop that one when they look away."

The four men looked around tryin' to figure out where that nut had come from. When nobody was lookin' our way, Fran raised up, pulled her leather pouch with another hickory nut in it to her cheek, an' let go.

It flew true an' whacked the guy on his left cheek, droppin' him to his knees. He put his hand to his face, pulled it back, an' looked at the blood on it. Didn't take but a couple three seconds for the whole side of his face to be covered in blood.

She dropped back down behind our cover as me an' Hutch patted her back an' grinned at her.

We could hear them talk 'cause we were only 'bout fifty feet away.

"*Vas zur Hölle*?" He took out his hanky an' held it to his cheek as they looked around again.

Hutch took a quick shot at another an' his hit the man in the crotch. Must have gotten his tallywhacker, 'cause he hollered real loud an' grabbed his private parts.

Fran couldn't help herself an' she giggled.

One that looked like he was the leader pointed. "Iz zhoze *verdammt* kids!"

They all turned toward our bush.

"Uh-oh, let's get." I grabbed Fran's hand. "Stay with me, Red. Hutch, go left. We'll meet at the honey tree."

"Gotcha." He took off like a turpentined cat, dodgin' through the woods.

The honey tree was a big ol' partly hollow oak tree that had a humongous bee hive inside—been there for years. Grandpa showed it to us last year when he went in to gather some honey—an' how to do it without makin' 'em mad. 'Course that also means we knew how to really stir 'em up.

Me an' Fran hauled butt back to the right a little, but still takin' 'em away from Unka Dud's cabin.

We could hear them men runnin' through the brush, tryin' to catch us. One of 'em got hung up in a whoa vine an' fell to his face in the leaves. The others had to stop an' help get him loose. Gave us a little runnin' room.

They didn't know much 'bout the woods an' 'specially them vines...the thorns on 'em will rip you up some. They're a bunch bigger than those on dewberry vines.

You can't go through 'em, they're green an' too tough, you have to step on 'em an' press 'em to the ground out of the way. We still try to avoid 'em whenever we can when we're out squirrel huntin' or somethin'.

We could see when we glanced back their way, they had their guns out, so we made sure to always keep some big trees 'tween us an' them.

Hutch musta looped back a bit an' took a shot 'cause one of 'em grabbed his ear an' yelled bloody murder. Burns like fire to get popped on the ear with somethin'—'specially a marble or a hickory nut from a sling shot.

When the whole bunch turned an' headed his way, me an' Fran both got in some licks 'fore we cut an' took off again.

We looked at each other while we ran an' giggled. We could hear 'em cussin', I guess in German. She'd got one on the hiney an' I hit another in the back of his head, knockin' his hat a flyin'.

Guess they figured out we were separated, 'cause they did the same thing. Two of 'em chased on after Hutch an' the other two, after us.

There was a branch near four feet deep I knew 'bout, so me an' Fran headed that way. It was too wide to jump, but there was a sweet gum tree that had fallen 'cross it an' we always used that—so did the coons, possums, an' bobcats—probably a panther once in a while, too.

The coons are pretty smart 'cause sometimes they tended to leave a little pile of scat on the log to cause whatever might be chasin' 'em to step in it—it's slicker'n snot on a doorknob when it's fresh.

When we got to the branch, we bent a bit to the left to where the log was. "Get right behind me, Red, an' don't step on any of that coon scat."

Glad she'd been takin' tumblin' an' stuff 'cause that log was only 'bout six inches in diameter. Wadn't much different'n walkin' on a train track rail, though.

"Don't worry about me."

We tippy-toed 'cross it an' found a good thick, leafy, shin oak to hide behind an' watch—they grew fairly low to the ground.

THE POND

The two that was chasin' us charged up to that branch, looked about, saw the log an' headed to it.

Yep, sure as the world, the one in the front stepped on some fresh coon scat an' just like steppin' on ice, his foot come out from under him an' he hit the water with a splash.

I nudged Fran to take a shot at the other one who had stopped an' was lookin' down in the water at his friend. She pulled back an' ricocheted a marble off his knee cap.

He hollered, his foot slipped off the log an' he dropped straight down, straddlin' that six inch log. He squealed like a half grown shoat, grabbed his crotch, an' slowly fell sideways like spit runnin' down a wall to hit the water next to his pal.

Me an' Fran hugged.

"Good shot, pard."

"I was aiming for the other knee."

"Six of one half dozen the other...Let's go."

We glanced back as we turned to run to see the two men, lookin' like drowned rats, crawl up the slick sides of the branch, slippin' back down several times 'fore they made it. They looked for us an' I guess I was gettin' a bit cocky an' leaned out from that shin oak an' waved at 'em—liked to have got myself shot.

The first one out was still on his knees by the bank. He pointed his Luger our way an' squeezed off a shot. The bullet clipped a limb right over my head.

Fran elbowed me as I ducked. "That wasn't bright."

I grabbed her hand again as we took off, keepin' that bush between us an' them. "Wanted to make sure we didn't lose 'em."

"Uh-huh." She looked at me out of the corner of her eye. "Wonder how Hutch is doing?"

"He knows these woods better'n I do. 'Spect he'll beat us to the honey tree…Speakin' of which, maybe it's time to lose these two."

"How? You've got them right on our tails."

I grinned at her. "Not for long."

We came to an old gully an' scooted down the side to the bottom. There was a shallow little branch down there.

"We'll take this puppy to the right. They won't know which way we went."

"They'll have a fifty-fifty chance of guessing correctly, won't they?"

THE POND

I glanced over at her as we splashed along in the water. "You didn't have to bring that up."

She shrugged. "Well…"

We came to another draw that branched off to the left an' took that—stopped for a second to listen.

"Nothin'…Musta gone the other way."

"For now."

I glanced at her again. "Would you quit…Don't pay to be negative."

She shrugged her shoulders.

I held up my hand to stop when we climbed out of the gully. "Uh-oh." I pulled her over behind a big ol' cottonwood. "Think we got us some problems."

"What?"

I pointed through the woods.

Fran followed my finger an' could see Hutch standin' beside a big old oak. He was bein' held by the other two men. One of his eyes was almost swole shut. Both the men had knots on their faces, some with blood runnin' from 'em.

I could hear the noise of somebody runnin' through the woods behind us—so could Fran.

"They must have figured out they went the wrong way and doubled back."

I nodded an' looked at her. "Think we're 'tween a rock an' a hard place, Red."

§§§

CHAPTER TWENTY-THREE

CABIN IN WOODS

Eric's head snapped up from the Edgar Rice Burroughs novel he was reading in his brown leather wing back chair by lantern light and the light from a nearby window. He removed his wire-rimmed glasses and cocked his head, listening for more sounds like he just heard—nothing.

"Zat vas a gunshot…from a pistol, Gauner." He stroked an orange tabby in his lap looking up at him from being disturbed from his nap. "Small caliber…Vas probably a .9mm…You zink?"

Gauner yawned, stretched his front paws and made mash on the arm of the chair.

Eric bookmarked the page in his copy of *At The Earth's Core,* published in 1922, and laid it on the end table beside his chair. He got to his feet, turned around and laid Gauner on the still warm seat where he promptly went back to sleep.

He opened the drawer in the narrow table, retrieved his German Luger PO8, checked the magazine, popped it back, and stuck the weapon in the belt at his waist.

After placing his battered fedora on his head, he exited the thick plank door of the spacious log cabin his brothers and he had built into the side of a low hill in 1915.

He didn't bother locking it as the secluded structure was well hidden deep in the woods, accessible only by an old, grown over, logging road that wound around in a circuitous pattern, like those roads did, for several miles before getting to the cabin.

THE POND

Eric Hoffer knew every inch of the woods surrounding his home and headed toward his spring fed lake known to the local kids as Uncle Dud's pond. The only ones that could get to it were Big John Jamison's grand kids from his property.

I figured we were almost a half-mile from the pond. I put my head close to Fran's ear.

"Shhh, Red, come on, let's go this way...got an idea."

"Uh-oh."

I looked back at her an' frowned, then turned, an' we slipped through the woods to the right. We got what I calculated as 'bout halfway around the small clearing an' found a real thick juniper we could get behind an' still see Hutch, them men, an' the tree.

I pulled out my sling shot an' nodded at Fran to take hers out, too. She wrinkled her brow on account she was confused as to what I had in mind—I wadn't though.

I held up a finger indicatin' to wait till I nodded. She shrugged, followed my lead, an' loaded one of our good clear marbles in her pouch—an' waited.

Hutch was strugglin' 'cause each man was holdin' an arm. Knew why he was doin' it. He was figurin' if he could get one arm loose, he could do that hip toss judo thing we'd worked on, but they wadn't havin' none of it—it was the same two we'd had truck with before at the house.

One of the men, with a swole up, bloody ear, slapped the fire out of him an' I had to grab Fran to keep her from runnin' in there an' jumpin' on him.

I mouthed. "Wait."

There was fire in her eyes when she turned an' glared at me. I just shook my head an' held up a finger again.

We could hear those two men that had been chasin' us comin' through the woods makin' enough noise to wake the dead. Course they didn't know we'd veered off an' they run right into that little openin' where Hutch an' them was next to that big oak tree.

Fran glared at me again, madder'n a wet hen 'cause now there was four to deal with. I just held my finger.

THE POND

When them two got to the tree with the others we could hear them ask if they'd seen us. The guys holdin' Hutch shook their heads. The other two looked around at the woods but couldn't see us.

I nudged Fran an' pointed up that oak 'bout ten or twelve feet to a hole dang near a foot in diameter. I made a soft buzzin' sound.

Her eyes got big as a pie plate—think she just figured out what we were goin' to do. I grinned an' nodded.

I squatted down so she could stand behind me, pulled my rubbers back far as they'd go right up 'gainst my cheek an' aimed for that hole. Fran did the same over my head.

When I nodded, we both let loose. Could hear those marbles whackin' around inside that hollow. Didn't take no time an' those bees come pouring out of that hole, madder'n blue blazes—somebody was fixin' to pay for messin' with their hive.

Fran leaned down to me. "What about Hutch?"

I grinned again. "Those bees will go after the biggest things livin' around...an' that's them men. Watch. Hutch knows what to do."

That swarm of bees was humongous an' was so thick it looked like a thunder cloud. Could hear 'em from where we were. Sounded like a squadron of bombers in one of those war movies.

Like I figured, the bees went after them four big men with a fury. They commenced to swattin', hollerin', an' runnin' 'round wavin' their arms. Like daddy would say, 'Didn't know whether to crap or go blind'.

When those two holdin' Hutch turned loose of him to fight that swarm of bees stingin' 'em, he hauled his bohunkus in the direction of the pond. Like I figured, the bees wadn't botherin' him none—they were after bigger game.

I grabbed Fran's hand an' we headed in the direction of the pond, too.

Seems like those Germans didn't have any more idea than a guinea in a thunderstorm where they were an' headed in the opposite direction, back the way me an' Fran had come. They were wavin' their arms about their heads tryin' to keep from gettin' stung. It wadn't workin'.

I giggled. They were gonna be lost as gooses an' with the bees right on their tails. Bees'll chase a thing for a half mile or better if they're mad enough—think we made sure these would be.

"How'd you know that would happen?"

THE POND

I glanced at Fran as we ran. "It's a gift."

She reached over an' thumped me.

We worked our way through those thick woods till we came out at the bank of the pond. Course we were on the other side from where we found those skeletons, but be easy enough to walk around the bank.

Fran poked me when I came out from behind a big thick cottonwood right after her. She pointed. Yep, there was Hutch, sittin' on a log next to the water with Unka Dud cleanin' the blood from his face an' placin' his folded up hanky soaked in that cold water from the pond on his eye. They musta popped him good. We ran up to 'em.

"You awright, Hutch?"

He looked up at us with his one good eye an' grinned. "Am now…Dang good idea you had, Foot. Knew right off what ya'll were doin' when I heard those marbles rattlin' around inside that holler tree." He laughed. "But they didn't. Lord have mercy at that black cloud of bees that swarmed out of that hole…Whooo-boy!"

Unka Dud smiled. "Would loved to have seen that." He looked around back toward the direction we'd come from. "Where do you think they are?"

Me an' Fran both giggled.

"Could well be in Louisiana, the direction they were runnin', Unka Dud."

He looked down at Hutch's face, turned it one way, then another with his finger. "How's zat eye feel now, son?"

Hutch looked at me an' grinned. "Oh, had a worst place on my lip an' never quit whistlin'." He knew that was one of my favorite expressions I had gotten from my daddy.

Unka Dud glanced up as Mister Tom came out of the woods on the other side of the pond.

Me, Fran, an' Hutch looked up too an' we waved as he jogged around the bank our way.

Didn't take long for him to get where we were.

"You kids okay?...Heard a gunshot."

Unka Dud nodded.

I kinda shrugged. "Uh...well, one of 'em shot at me, but he missed."

Fran rolled her eyes an' I glanced at her. "We made 'em fall in that branch back yonder through the woods. They weren't very happy 'bout it."

Then we told him 'bout sicin' the bees on 'em an' the other stuff...

THE POND

"So, when we came out of the woods, Unka Dud was doctorin' on Hutch's shiner."

"I heard vhat must have been ze same shot, Tom, and headed zhis vay from ze cabin." He looked over me an' Fran's shoulder into the woods. "Looks like zhey are getting close to finding me."

"We came to tell you, Unka Dud, that it was possible they had seen you headin' this way when you left grandpa's house last night...They were already at the pond when we came up." I looked at Fran an' Hutch. "We thought we'd lead 'em deeper into the bottom an' get 'em lost."

Fran smiled an' elbowed me. "Don't think they had any bread crumbs to leave for a trail."

Unka Dud nodded an' smiled. "Ah, like ze fairy tale of Hansel and Gretel...Vell, you may have done zhat...for now. Come, ve vill go to ze cabin. I have zome fresh peach strrrr-udel."

He kinda rolled his 'r's when he said that.

Hutch looked at Unka Dud with his good eye. "What's strudel?"

Unka Dud laughed. "You shall see, young man, you shall see."

The four Germans finally stopped almost a mile from the oak tree hive. Each one bent over and put his hands on their knees trying to breathe.

Not a single one escaped the wrath of the honey bees. They had lost their hats, and their faces, necks, hands, and even the tops of their heads were misshapen and all covered with lumps caused by bee stings.

Amell's eyes were almost completely swollen shut. "*Diese verdammten kinder*…ve kill zhem next time."

Jonas looked around at the surrounding dense woods, then at Amell. "If zhere iz a next time. Ve are lost."

§§§

CHAPTER TWENTY-FOUR

CABIN IN WOODS

Unka Dud fixed us a plate with what he called a strudel. It was dang near as big around as my calf an' was a kind of biscuit dough rolled up with peach jam stuff in between the layers an' cooked a golden brown. He heated 'em up a little in his stove warmer an' put a dollop of butter on top—um-um-um. Went great with the buttermilk he got out of his cold room he had gotten from grandma.

Hutch took a bite. "Lord have mercy an' bless all the little children...This is some kinda good, Unka Dud."

He grinned. "Thought you might like it."

Fran shook her head, slingin' her long pony tail from side to side. "That's not the half of it...This is awesome." She stuck another forkful in her mouth.

I started to take another bite myself when we heard a rollin' rumble from outside an' the light comin' through the windows went way down.

Unka Dud's cat, Gauner, looked up at the ceilin', then went back to sleep in the chair he was in.

"Looks like a storm brewing." Mister Tom glanced outside through a window.

Unka Dud nodded. "Goot, maybe it'll wash away any tracks we might have left toward ze cabin from ze pond."

I looked over at him an' Mister Tom between bites. "Maybe it'll wash them Germans away, too."

"I'm afraid they're too mean, Foot, but at least they'll be very uncomfortable out there in the rain."

THE POND

Mister Tom always had a logical outlook on things.

He turned to Unka Dud. "That's an interesting cold room, you have there, Eric."

Unka Dud glanced back at the book case that covered near two-thirds of the wall which was made out of a funny lookin' rock he called bauxite. It was kinda pink an' looked like it had chunks of other rocks in it.

His cold room, where he kept fruits, vegetables, meat, milk, an' cheese was dug back into the hill where he said it stayed 'bout fifty degrees most all the time. The door was a three foot section of the bookcase that would swing out. Couldn't tell for nothin' that it was there.

"*Ja*, Tom. My brothers and I drove our trucks up to Saline County, zhis zide of Little Rock, and got enough of zhat rock for ze vall and ze room inside ze hill. Ve lined ze cold room mit it and zen built shelves out of cypress."

Hutch looked up from his strudel. "How come ya'll to use rock 'stead of logs like the rest of the house?"

He smiled. "Ze logs, being vood, Hutch, vould rot in ze ground in a few years...zo ve used rock for it and ze foundation."

"Oh, guess that makes sense."

Fran nudged him. "See, Hutch, learn something every day, if you pay attention."

"I know that."

Fran looked at the big wide bookcase that went almost to the rafters cross the ceilin'. "You've got almost as many books as our library back in Kilgore, Uncle Dud."

"Books are my love, Frances. Vouldn't know vhat I vould do mitout zhem...I can travel ze vorld, zee lost cities, and even go to other planets, and inzide our own mit zhem."

Hutch's head snapped up again. "Inside our world?"

"*Ja*, Edgar Rice Burroughs wrote about a world inside ours called *Pellucidar*, and so did other writers, like Jules Verne, who wrote a book called *Journey to ze Center of ze Earth*...I have zhem both."

"Gol-uh-olee! Can I read some of 'em?"

He nodded an' shook his finger at Hutch. "*Ja*...if you promise to be very careful mit zhem."

THE POND

"Oh, yes, sir…Know all about that. Foot will thump my noggin' if I damage one of his."

"Goot."

Mister Tom turned his head an' listened to the continuous roll of thunder an' kinda smiled. "Sounds like a distant artillery battle."

Could tell he was rememberin' the war.

A bolt of lightning hit nearby with a really loud bang. Everbody jumped, 'cludin' Gauner—then the bottom fell out.

The downpour created a roar on the slate shingles on the roof of the cabin—but not near as loud as at grandma's when it rains on their tin roof.

Unka Dud got up an' put another log on the fire in his cast iron stove as another big bolt of lightnin' hit somewhere close.

The four men huddled miserably underneath a large cedar tree, hoping it wouldn't get hit by the frequent lightning. All four were still covered with knots and lumps from the bee stings.

The swelling around Amell's eyes had gone down enough that the others could see the fires of hatred burn in them.

"Ze vill die...all of zhem vhen ve find zhem. Including ze old man."

"Ve still need to find vhere he hid ze items, Amell."

He turned his burning eyes on Jonas. "I no longer care about zhem. You may ask him one time...zhen he dies...I vill not be made ze fool of...especially by zome znot-nosed children friends of zhat Gypsy Jew." He spat to the side. "Ve have done mitout zhose things for zirty-five years, ve can continue to do so...Zhey don't give us zhat much more power."

"Ze new Reich vill not be happy."

Amell glared at Jonas again. "Ze new Reich is not here...Come, ve are already vet. Let us zee about getting out of ziz place."

Jonas looked around. "Vhich vay?"

"It does not matter...Ve valk till ve get zomevhere."

They ducked their heads down and headed into the driving rain, weaving through the dense woods. The canopy above kept the undergrowth to a minimum.

THE POND

The wave of blowing rain seemed to be slackin' off some, least it wadn't pepperin' against the windows.

Unka Dud was showin' us some of the books in his collections. He had all of the books my favorite author, Edgar Rice Burroughs, wrote, almost seventy I think, an' all twenty-two of the Tarzan novels. That was all of 'em so far as I knew. I had twelve original hardback print copies an' the rest were paperbacks. He had *all* first printin's. I'm so jealous I can't see straight.

I got tickled when he said he'd read most of 'em two or three times—me, too.

Fran an' Hutch just stood there in front of the bookshelves, starin' at all the titles, their mouths hangin' open.

Think Mister Tom an' Unka Dud thought it was funny, too. An' Mister Tom had a bunch of books at his house, but not near as many as this.

Mama quit gettin' me the hardbacks an' went to the little paperbacks on account we moved so much an' the packin' started gettin' to be a real chore.

I pointed to a leather bound book with gold lettering for the title. "I never heard of this book or author…*Behind the Secret Door* by Archimedes Trent."

Unka Dud chuckled. "Das is my pen name an' ze book is a mystery I wrote. I put it zhere as a play on vords because behind it is vhere ze handle to open ze secret door to ze cold room is."

I grinned real big. "Oh, wow, that is so neat. Who would think?"

"*Ja*, my thoughts, too…Vould anyone like zome hot cocoa?"

We turned from lookin' at all the titles an' nodded. The rain had almost stopped an' the only sound was the water drippin' off the roof.

After moving the book aside, he opened the door, went inside the room an' came back out with a jug of milk to make the cocoa. He closed the secret door behind him with a soft click.

"Would you like some help, Uncle Dud?"

"Of course, Frances. Come right over here to ze counter and get zhat pan down, if you vould."

She reached up, got the pan hanging on a hook an' set it on the counter.

"Now zome cane sugar and zome goot German chocolate…"

THE POND

There was a pop from outside an' a thud against the three inch thick plank door at the front of the cabin.

"Hey, old man…Ve know you're in zhere. Come out or ve're coming in to get you."

The muffled voice came from outside somewhere. We knew who it was.

He looked at me, Fran, an' Hutch. "You children hide in ze cold room. Tom and I vill deal mit zhis."

We all looked at each other, shook our heads an' took our sling shots out.

Mister Tom came over an' stood in front of us. "Now, listen, kids, we appreciate you wanting to help…but they have guns."

I glanced at Fran an' Hutch. "Don't care, we can fight too." I held up my sling shot. "These are quiet. They won't know where they're comin' from."

"There's only three windows and…"

There was another shot an' another thud on the door. "You coming out, Bieler?"

§§§

CHAPTER TWENTY-FIVE

CABIN IN WOODS

"Vhat do ve do if he doesn't come out?"

Amell glared at Elias. "Ve burn him out."

"How? All ze wood is too vet."

Amell glanced up at the still gray drizzling sky, then at the log house, and then turned to his three sodden and bedraggled companions. "Zen ve slip up to ze three vindows and shoot inside. He can't cover zem all."

Amell pointed Jonas and Elias to the side of the cabin with two windows and Bernard to the side with one. He would cover the door. The four Germans slipped toward their assigned places.

Unka Dud eased up to the window on the east side an' closed the wooden shutters that were on the inside. There was a small diamond shaped hole when the two pieces were fastened together with a slidin' steel bolt.

Mister Tom headed to one of the windows on the front on one side of the door an' did the same, then stepped over to the other an' closed it, too.

"Ze vooden shutters are inch thick oak....a .9 millimeter bullet vill not penetrate it." He motioned Mister Tom to come to the west side.

"I don't understand, Eric, there are no windows on this side."

"*Ja*, ze vall you zee changes to rock and goes into ze hill." Unka Dud smiled. "But here is another of my hidden doors to ze outside."

We stared at where he pointed but couldn't see any door.

Unka Dud moved a picture of him an' his brothers when they were younger, guess 'bout the time they came here. It was hinged to the log wall an' behind it was a lever—he pulled it. A two foot wide section of the wall swung inside.

"Ze voodpile is beside ze door and hides it from view on ze outside. Ve put it zhere to get to ze voodpile mitout going out ze front door." His dark brown eyes twinkled. "And for zis very purpose, if ve needed it."

He nodded to Mister Tom, an' then turned to me. "Foot, close zis vhen ve leave, it vill automatically latch."

Mister Tom looked at me. "Ya'll stay put, hear?"

Him an' Unka Dud hunched over an' stepped through the openin'. I closed the door behind 'em an' sure 'nuff, it clicked in place an' the lever flipped back.

"Gol-uh-olee." Hutch shook his head.

Fran looked at me after they were gone. "Well? Are we?"

I grinned. "What do you think, Red?"

THE POND

"Uh-huh."

Hutch took a big breath. "Oh, Lordy."

"Since this is the back side from the front door…we go out an' duck into the woods 'cause they're real close back there. We spread out an' do what we did earlier with our sling shots…Stay outta sight."

"Easy for you to say, I got red hair."

I looked around the cabin. "Get one of Unka Dud's hats an' stuff your hair up under it."

Fran nodded. "That'll work."

She grabbed one of his old fedoras off a peg, put her pony tail on top of her head an' pulled the hat down to her ears.

Me an' Hutch both giggled at the way it made her ears stick out an' fold over.

"Hope they don't stay that way, Red."

Hutch cocked his head. "Look kinda like Mortimer Snerd."

She whacked us both as we went out the small door an' scooted to the woods.

I pointed Hutch to circle back around the hill to get on the far east side an' in front of the cabin. Me an' Fran went the other way, an' then split up.

We could move real quiet on account of the leaves on the ground bein' wet an' all.

Tom and Eric split up and positioned themselves on either side of the front of the cabin as the four Germans made their move forward.

Tom was on the two window side and Eric, the single window.

Tom started to rise up as Jonas and Elias moved toward the window.

Elias yelled out and grabbed his cheek as blood dripped between his fingers.

Jonas did the same, except he put his right hand over his ear after switching the gun to his left.

Tom looked around. "Those darn kids." He rose up, both hands wrapped around his Luger. "Far enough."

Jonas spun around quickly trying to get his pistol back in his shooting hand. He managed to snap off a couple of shots after making the change.

Tom had anticipated what the German would do, hit the ground, rolled over and double tapped him twice in the center of his chest. Jonas dropped where he stood.

THE POND

Elias fired twice at Tom, but he had already rolled back in the opposite direction.

Tom brought his gun to bear on the German when he got back to his stomach, but he had ducked back into the woods after firing at him. He heard three quick shots from across the way where Eric was—then silence.

No one moved. Each was waiting for someone to show themselves—then there was a *twhack* that sounded to Tom's left. It was followed instantly by a yelp of pain. He belly-crawled that direction.

Elias showed himself from around the opposite side of a hickory tree, turned and pointed a Beretta M9 back behind him.

Tom double tapped the side of Elias' head. Both holes appeared in front of his ear, less than a millimeter apart. He was dead before he hit the ground.

"Two down…hopefully three."

Fran crawled underneath a big cedar. I could see that leader of the Germans not ten feet in front of her but she couldn't. I drew my rubbers back an' let fly a marble. It bounced off his forehead which was still lumpy from the bee stings—had to hurt like the devil.

"Aiii!...*Verdammt*! He got to his feet wavin' his pistol around lookin' for anybody to shoot.

I turned an' saw Mister Tom step forward. "Drop it, or die."

The German spun back to his left an' pointed his gun at Mister Tom.

"He zaid drop it."

Unka Dud came out from behind a tree off to the right with his Luger aimed at him.

I got to my feet to watch an' the leader swung that black pistol at me.

"*Nein*." He flicked his eyes at Mister Tom, then at Unka Dud. "You drop yours or ze boy dies."

Mister Tom never took his eyes from that German, but spoke to Unka Dud, "You double tap his chest, I'll double tap his head."

Unka Dud grinned an' nodded. "*Ja*."

The German looked back at me, aimin' his gun right at my face—could see his finger tightenin' on the trigger.

The whole woods seemed to explode with one giant roar. When I opened my eyes back up, the German had fallen backwards right where he stood—dead as a hammer. There were two holes in his chest and two in his head. Mister Tom an' Unka Dud had each fired twice, but it sounded like only one shot.

The woods went quiet again. Fran crawled out from under the cedar an' I could see Hutch comin' from across the way as we all approached the dead German.

Mister Tom an' Unka Dud walked up to his body.

"That's all of them, Eric." Mister Tom stared at the body.

Unka Dud nodded. "Goot."

Then he dropped his Luger by his foot and collapsed to the ground, face down.

Mister Tom rushed over to him, knelt down an' gently rolled him over. We could all see a red stain growin' on his chest.

"Get his weapon, Foot." He jerked a handkerchief from his pocket, folded it into a pad, ripped Unka Dud's shirt open an' pressed it over the hole that was oozin' blood.

He turned to Fran. "Keep your hand on this, Frances, I'm going to pick him up and carry him back to the cabin.

Her eyes were huge, but she did what he asked.

Mister Tom picked him up like he was a child and walked fast as he could to the cabin.

It was a good thing I hadn't closed that little door on account the front door was locked.

"Hutch! Run ahead, get back inside through that little door an' open the front one for Mister Tom."

"Got it."

He took off like his hair was on fire an' disappeared around the back side of the cabin. Didn't take no time till the front door swung open.

Mister Tom carried Unka Dud inside an' laid him on his bed. "Find me some towels. Gotta stop this bleeding…if it's not too late."

Fran brought a stack of clean towels. Mister Tom peeled the rest of Unka Dud's bloody shirt off an' slung it to the side.

I laid the guns I picked up, includin' Unka Dud's, on the table.

"Is he gonna be awright, Mister Tom?"

He pressed a clean folded up towel over the wound an' bit his lower lip. "I don't know, Foot, I don't know…He's not breathing good."

THE POND

We all gathered around the bed while Mister Tom worked on him. Even his cat, Gauner, had raised up with his front paws on the side of the bed, watchin'.

"Get some water, Frances, wash his face and wipe some of this blood around this towel away." He slung that one to the floor an' put another on his chest.

Unka Dud's lids fluttered an' he looked up. He reached an' grabbed Mister Tom's shirt, his eyes had a pleadin' look to 'em.

"Must…must protec…"

Then his hand relaxed an' fell back to the bed as his eyes closed again…

§§§

CHAPTER TWENTY-SIX

CABIN IN WOODS

"Is he...?" I looked over at Mister Tom.

He shook his head. "No...not yet, at least. His breathing is real shallow, but he's a tough old bird...Need to get him out of here and to a doctor. That bullet needs to come out...and soon."

"Reckon that old truck outside runs?"

THE POND

"Doesn't matter, Foot. That loggin' road that leads here winds around too much and would be way too rough…It would kill him sure."

"What are we going to do?" Fran had tears in her eyes as she looked from Unka Dud to Mister Tom.

He set his mouth, an' then looked at us. "Take him out of here up to John's house. It's only about a mile."

I raised my eyebrows a little. "How?"

"I'll carry him."

"All the way?"

Mister Tom nodded. "All the way. He's a warrior and my friend…Frances, rip up a sheet so I can wrap it around his chest to hold that pad to the wound." He looked at me an' Hutch. "Which one of ya'll are the best runner?"

I pointed at Hutch. "By a bunch."

He nodded. "Hutch, you run on ahead to John's house, ya'll go over to Smead's store, and call the sheriff and Doctor Duckworth. Tell 'em what happened and to come out and hurry…and send an ambulance. Now scat. We'll meet you at John's."

Hutch headed to the door. "I'm gone."

Fran took a sheet from Unka Dud's linen cabinet an' ripped a long piece 'bout eight inches wide. She rolled it up an' handed it to Mister Tom.

"Thanks, now help me wrap this around him while I hold him up."

"Yessir."

She started wrappin' it around Unka Dud while Mister Tom cradled his head an' helped Fran keep the cloth tight. When they finished, Mister Tom picked him up in his arms, leanin' Unka Dud's head against his shoulder.

"Get the door, Frances…Foot, put some food and water out for Gauner, and then catch up to us."

Fran held the door open as Mister Tom carried him through an' headed toward grandpa's.

I fed an' watered Gauner, an' it didn't take no time to catch up, even though Mister Tom was really stridin' out. He was bein' extra careful to not shake Unka Dud around much.

I got to the fence first, put my foot on the third wire an' Fran an' me both lifted the second one up high as we could to give him plenty of room to step through. He was carryin' Unka Dud like he was nothin'.

THE POND

We'd just started 'cross grandpa's pasture when we saw him an' daddy hustlin' our way. Guess daddy shut the rig down when the storm came up.

"Here, Tom, let me carry him." Daddy took Unka Dud an' headed up the hill.

"You all right, Tom?"

He put his hands on his knees for a moment or so, then straightened up, an' they started walkin' to catch up to daddy.

"I'm fine, John, but am glad ya'll showed up. My gas was starting to run low.

We could see the sheriff's car an' the ambulance pull into the front of the house. Doctor Duckworth was in the car with the sheriff.

I ran on ahead an' opened the gate for daddy.

"Where do you want him, Doc?"

"Bring him up to the ambulance, Joe. I want to do a quick examination then we'll head to town."

"Bullet's still in there, Doc."

"Thanks, Tom."

Pete an' Charlie had the back of the ambulance open an' a stretcher in the middle. They would put it, with Unka Dud, in the web supports on the side when the doctor was done.

There was some kind of clear bag hangin' on the side with a long skinny tube attached. Guess it was some kinda medicine for somebody hurt or shot. A green tank like, a miniature weldin' tank, was hooked to the side, too. There was a mask thing attached to it. Think that musta been oxygen.

Pete stuck that tube from the bag to Unka Dud's arm—had some kinda needle on the end. Then Charlie put the mask thing over Unka Dud's face while the doc was checkin' him over.

He took the stethoscope ends from his ears an' turned to Pete an' Charlie. "Get him secured an' lets get him to town...stat!"

Now I don't know exactly what that 'stat' word means, but I'm guessin' it's somethin' like 'get the lead out'.

They stuck the stretcher in that webbin' stuff on the side an' buckled it in. The doc crawled up in the back of the ambulance to be with Unka Dud. They shut an' latched the doors, got in, an' roared off—lights an' sirens a goin'.

Mister Tom watched 'em leave. "I pray to God they get there in time...He's a hellova man."

Grandpa put his arm around Tom's shoulders an' led him up to the house.

THE POND

They sat down in the rockers on the porch an' grandma an' mama brought out cups of coffee for him, grandpa, daddy, an' the sheriff.

Mister Tom had some coffee, leaned back, closed his eyes for a minute, then he looked at the sheriff.

"When Pete an' Charlie come back out, I'll lead 'em to that road that goes to Eric's and to those four stiffs we left down there.

He nodded. "They ain't goin' nowhere, don't imagine."

Tiny came out with them an' laid down next to my feet. Could tell she was feelin' some better.

Grandpa took a sip, an' then looked at me. "Think you've got some explainin' to do, Foot."

Daddy looked at him an' raised one eyebrow.

Grandpa looked over at him. "Told them not to go to the pond." He looked back at me. "And that's exactly where they went."

His eyes were burnin' a hole through me.

"Sometime today, boy."

"Uh…well…uh, wadn't sure which pond you meant, Grandpa."

"Bull crap…Nice try."

I glanced at Hutch an' Fran. "And we…"

279

"What do you mean, 'we'?"

"Awright, I…"

"We coulda said no, cuz."

I glanced at Fran an' nodded. Knew she'd jump in.

"Just felt it was important that Unka Dud knew them Germans might have seen which way he went."

Fran nodded. "Turns out, that's just what happened."

"It's a good thing they did, too."

We all looked at Mister Tom.

"They kept that bunch on the run with their sling shots till I could get down there…even got that whole honey bee hive in that big oak after 'em and got 'em lost…at least for a while.

'Bout fifteen minutes later, Mister Tom finished tellin' grandpa an' daddy what all happened.

"…I'm thinking neither Eric nor I would be around at all if they hadn't, John." He looked at me. "They were real Marines…Improvise, adapt, and overcome." Mister Tom saluted us.

THE POND

Had to bite my lip to keep from cryin'. I came to attention, like we were taught in the Cub Scouts, an' saluted him back—so did Fran an' Hutch.

Grandpa an' daddy exchanged glances. I could tell daddy was tryin' not to smile—wadn't workin'.

"They still need to be punished for not minding, Joe." Grandpa cleared his throat.

"I agree, John. What do you have in mind?"

He turned that steely gaze to us. "Tomorrow, I want ya'll to completely clean out Sally and Ted's stalls and put all new clean hay in 'em."

Wow, we lucked out...Wadn't goin' to get a bustin'.

The sheriff glanced at Mister Tom. "Ever find out what those Germans were after?"

He shook his head. "Nope...no idea. They just think Eric, or I guess it's Motshan Bieler, has it hidden somewhere. "

It was almost a week later, me, Fran, an' Hutch were playin' cars under the sycamore trees out front. She was scheduled to catch the bus back to Kilgore, day after tomorrow—sure gonna miss her.

We looked up as the sheriff pulled up an' stopped in front. He got out an' the passenger door on the other side opened. Son of a gun, it was Unka Dud. His right arm was in some kinda sling, guess from the hospital.

They came in the gate an' we ran up to him clamorin' around him. He looked a little peaked, but was movin' awright.

"Unka Dud, you're awright."

"Hi, children. *Ja*, I have been better, but it beats the alternative." He smiled. "Ze doctor didn't have to dig around for ze bullet...it vas lodged against my shoulder blade."

Mister Tom came out the screen door as we stepped up on the porch. "Eric, or is suppose I should say Motshan..."

"I zink I'd prefer Eric, Tom. Haven't used Motshan for thirty-five years." He glanced at me, Fran, an' Hutch. "Or Uncle Dud iz still fine."

We grinned 'cause we were used to it, too.

Grandpa pointed to a rocker. "Have a seat...Eric."

He looked at grandpa, then the rest of us. "I zink I'd like to go out to my place. Need to see to Gauner..."

THE POND

"I've been going out there, feeding and watering him every day, Eric. Talking to him for a while, too."

He nodded. "You are a goot friend, Tom. Zank you." He looked at us again. "Zhere is zomthing I need to show you."

Mister Tom kinda cocked his head. "Now?"

"*Ja*...It is time."

"You up for the walk?"

Unka Dud looked at the sheriff.

"*Ja*, ve go slow. Been on my back for a week...Need ze exercise."

Grandpa turned to us. "Why don't you kids stay here."

"*Nein*, John, zhey need to zee, too." He stepped over an' put his good arm around us as we pressed up against him. "Zhey are special to me."

Mister Tom nodded. "Well, let'itys go then."

He led our little parade over to the gate to the pasture an' down toward the woods between here an' Unka Dud's pond.

When we got to the cabin, Gauner wouldn't stop rubbin' back an forth 'tween Unka Dud's legs an' purrin' loud enough to be heard outside. Think he was glad Unka Dud was home.

He stepped over an' nodded to Mister Tom to open the bookcase to the cold room an' led us inside.

There were two wooden cases of potatoes an' onions that he pointed to. "Tom, if you an' Joe vould move zhese an' zhen lift up zhat ring you zee underneath."

They got 'em moved out of the way an' daddy lifted the iron ring set into a kinda recess in the floor. A trap door on springs came up an' there was a stairway underneath.

Unka Dud was holdin' a coal oil lantern an' he led the way down the stairs to another room. It was a lot like the cold room. The rock walls were lined with cypress shelves—the floor was of a flat rock that looked like the same stuff his roof was, slate.

His good arm swept around the room which was I figured was 'bout twelve by twelve.

"Zhis is vhat ze Germans are after—our treasure."

We looked around and there was just shelves with wooden cases lined up in 'em like it was a pantry.

"Zhere is zome gold an' jewels." He indicated several boxes stacked around. "But zhat is not ze main zhing." He pointed to a wooden case for Tom to pick up. "Open it, please, Tom."

He opened it an' there were some rolled up paper lookin' stuff.

"Zhese scrolls are books zhat vere removed from ze original Bible. Ze church father, a Athanasius of Alexandra, removed all books mit referencing vomen as equal to men in 367 AD...Ze Book of Lilith, zat vas Adams first vife, she vas created from ze zame dust as Adam but refused to be subservant to him. She left ze Garden of Eden...zo Gott made Eve...from Adam's rib."

I looked around an' everbody's mouth, includin' mine were hangin' open.

"Zhis is ze Book of Enoch..."

Daddy frowned. "Why was it removed?"

"Ze early Jews removed it because it contained prophecies pertaining to Christ and zhey considered it apocryphal."

"What's that, Unka Dud?"

"Zhat means zhey didn't zhink it came from Gott...A matter of opinion, I suppose." He pointed to some more cases. "Zhese are ze original texts of ze Gospel According to Mary…"

"Is that the mother of Jesus?"

"No, Frances, zhis vould be Mary Magdalene…considered to be one of Jesus disciples an' believe to be his favorite…possibly even his vife."

"Gol-uh-olee."

"Ze Gospel of Thomas, ze Gospel of Philip, and nine others…all because zhey showed vomen equal to men and zherefore not ze vord of Gott."

Mister Tom pointed to a kind of fancy box with brass fittin's. "And that?"

"Please pick it up…and be very careful. Hold it out in both arms."

Mister Tom did as he was told.

Unka Dud opened the two clasps at the front. "Zhis vood is called gopher vood. Legend has it zhat zhis box vaz made from vood from Noah's Ark."

There was a sort of hissin' sound as everbody took a breath.

Unka Dud lifted the lid. Inside was what looked to me like the end of a iron knife or spear layin' on a pad of red silk lookin' stuff.

THE POND

"Zhis is the broken point of ze The Holy Lance, also known as ze Lance of Longinus…"

Mister Tom whispered. "The spear of the Roman soldier that pierced Christ's side."

"*Ja*, he vas seeing if he vas dead yet."

"We read 'bout that in Sunday school."

Grandpa was finally able to speak, "This was what Hitler spent years searchin' for…along with the Ark of the Covenant. Thought it would give the Third Reich great spiritual power to conquer the world."

"*Ja*…Ze point vas said to have been broken off vhen Jerusalem vas captured by ze Persian forces of King Khosrau II in 615. Ze story goes, it vas vas given Nicetas, who took it to Constantinople vhere it vas placed ze Church of the Virgin of ze Pharos…Zhis point of ze lance vas put in zhis box of gopher vood and vas acquired by ze Latin Emperor Baldwin II of Constantinople, who zold it to Louis IX of France."

Daddy leaned over an' studied the end of the spear. "What about the rest of it."

"Ve zhink it is at Saint Peter's Basilica in Rome, out of reach of ze Nazis…Zhis piece vas enshrined mit ze crown of thorns in ze Sainte

Chapelle in Paris and disappeared during ze French Revolution in ze 1700s...My people got it or rescued it, if you vill. Ve vill not allow it to be misused...It has ze blood of our Lord on it."

Mister Tom looked at him. "It that when your sect converted to Christianity?"

He shook his head. "Mine family vere born Jews. Ve joined the Gypsy clan in ze 1400s...Zhat is when ve became Christians."

Grandpa turned to him. "Why show these valuable relics to us?"

"Mit my brothers gone. I am ze end of ze line of protectors...I have met many people in my life and you are ze only ones I can trust. I don't have too many years left in zhis life...Zomeone must protect zhese zings for our Lord."

Me, Hutch, an' Fran looked at each other, then at grandpa, the sheriff, an' daddy. They didn't know what to say either. All I could think of was..."Oboy."

§§§§§

PREVIEW

the Next Exciting
Foot & Hutch Story

FRIENDS

CHAPTER ONE

JAMISON HOME

"Hutch is what?"

I stared at grandpa while I warmed my behind at the fire at the fireplace. Tiny was curled up on the rag rug next to me, warmin' herself at the fire, too.

He leaned forward in his rocker an' spat a long yellow stream of snuff juice into the fire. It splattered on a burnin' log an' sizzled for a minute before burnin' away. Me an' Tiny made sure we were on the side of the big wide fireplace so grandpa had plenty of room to spit in the fire.

"The sheriff has him in for questioning on some burglaries in the area...and a murder. An older widow woman."

I was stunned. We'd just got there from Fort Morgan, Colorado, where daddy had been transferred to from Junction City, Arkansas, a couple months ago.

It was two weeks before Christmas an' daddy decided to take his vacation at Shell Oil to come to southern Arkansas in the winter to get away from the snow an' ice in Colorado where they'd been drillin' for oil—didn't work.

It was cold as the dickens when we got here, with snow expected—yea.

Mister Tom had moved into the cabin down in the woods near the pond with Unka Dud as he was still recouperatin' from the gunshot wound he got when we tangled with those Germans last summer.

We had all been tasked by Unka Dud to help take care of the secret treasure he'd been guardin' for thirty-five years.

"There ain't no way Hutch ever robbed anybody…much less a killin'. No way!"

Grandpa nodded. "I know, I know, Foot. We all are aware Hutch wouldn't do something like this." He spat again an' wiped the dribble from his chin. "But someone said they saw him at old Missus Rigg's house…the lady that got killed."

"At it or near it?"

"That's a good point, Foot. We'll have to find out…There have been a number of burglaries around here, but apparently, this time the owner, in this case, Widow Riggs, walked in on 'em. Her daughter, who lives 'bout a half mile away, found her…She'd been beaten to death."

Mama put her hand over her mouth. "My God."

"See, now there you go. No way a ten year old like me or Hutch can beat a woman to death…no way."

Grandpa kinda grimaced. "Whoever did it apparently used a club or stick, Foot."

Daddy sat down in another rocker in front of the fireplace. It was the only heat in the house 'cause they still didn't have electricity. The co-op had promised, but still nothin'.

"What's the thief stealing, John?"

FRIENDS

Grandpa still carried a deputy sheriff's badge an' the sheriff called on him for help from time to time.

"I investigated several of the robberies myself, Joe, an' the usual stuff...cash, jewelry and the like. I think they watch the house and the mail delivery then pick the week after they know the owner gets a check an' has the time to go to town to the bank and cash it."

"Sounds a little sophisticated for a ten year old boy, doesn't it?"

"I'd say."

Grandma came in the parlor. "Vertis, come help me bring the coffee and cocoa in."

"All right, Mama."

My mom got up an' followed grandma down the wide dog run to the kitchen.

"How many witnesses saw Hutch?"

Grandpa looked from daddy to me. "One."

My mouth fell open. "One?...And how did they describe him?"

"Colored boy, nine or ten, short nappy hair..."

Daddy rolled his eyes.

§§

AUTHOR

Ken Farmer didn't write his first full novel until he was sixty-nine years of age. He often wonders what the hell took him so long. At age seventy-nine...he's currently working on novel number forty.

Ken spent thirty years raising cattle and quarter horses in Texas and forty-five years as a professional actor (after a stint in the Marine Corps). Those years gave him a background for storytelling...or as he has been known to say, "I've always been a bit of a bull---t artist, so writing novels kind of came naturally once it occurred to me I could put my stories down on paper."

Ken's writing style has been likened to a combination of Louis L'Amour and Terry C. Johnston with an occasional Hitchcockian twist...now that's a combination.

In addition to his love for writing fiction, he likes to teach acting, voice-over and writing workshops. His favorite expression is: "Just tell the damn story."

Writing has become Ken's second life: he has been a Marine, played collegiate football, been a Texas wildcatter, cattle and horse rancher, professional film and TV actor and director, and now...a novelist. Who knew?

Ken Farmer's dialogue flows like a beautiful western river...it's the gold standard...Carole Beers

OTHER NOVELS FROM
TIMBER CREEK PRESS

MILITARY ACTION/TECHNO
BLACK EAGLE FORCE: Eye of the Storm (Book #1)
by Buck Stienke and Ken Farmer
BLACK EAGLE FORCE: Sacred Mountain (Book #2) by Buck Stienke and Ken Farmer
RETURN of the STARFIGHTER (Book #3)
by Buck Stienke and Ken Farmer
BLACK EAGLE FORCE: BLOOD IVORY (Book #4)
by Buck Stienke and Ken Farmer with Doran Ingrham
BLACK EAGLE FORCE: FOURTH REICH (Book #5) by Buck Stienke and Ken Farmer
AURORA: INVASION (Book #6 in the BEF) by Ken Farmer & Buck Stienke
BLACK EAGLE FORCE: ISIS (Book #7) by Buck Stienke and Ken Farmer
BLOOD BROTHERS - Doran Ingrham, Buck Stienke and Ken Farmer
DARK SECRET - Doran Ingrham
NICARAGUAN HELL - Doran Ingrham
BLACKSTAR BOMBER by T.C. Miller
BLACKSTAR BAY by T.C. Miller

BLACKSTAR MOUNTAIN by T.C. Miller
BLACKSTAR ENIGMA by T.C. Miller

HISTORICAL FICTION WESTERN

THE NATIONS by Ken Farmer and Buck Stienke
HAUNTED FALLS by Ken Farmer and Buck Stienke
HELL HOLE by Ken Farmer
ACROSS the RED by Ken Farmer and Buck Stienke
BASS and the LADY by Ken Farmer and Buck Stienke
DEVIL'S CANYON by Buck Stienke
LADY LAW by Ken Farmer
BLUE WATER WOMAN by Ken Farmer
FLYNN by Ken Farmer
AURALI RED by Ken Farmer
COLDIRON by Ken Farmer
STEELDUST by Ken Farmer
BONE by Ken Farmer
BONE'S LAW by Ken Farmer
BONE & LORAINE by Ken Farmer
BONE'S GOLD by Ken Farmer
BONE'S ENIGMA by Ken Farmer
SILKE JUSTICE by Ken Farmer
SILKE'S QUEST by Ken Farmer
NO TIME to DIE by Buck Stienke

SILKE'S RIDE by Ken Farmer
ANGEL JUSTICE by Ken Farmer
SKINWALKER JUSTICE by Ken Farmer

SY/FY
LEGEND of AURORA by Ken Farmer & Buck Stienke
AURORA: INVASION (Book #6 in the BEF) by Ken Farmer & Buck Stienke

HISTORICAL FICTION ROMANCE
THE TEMPLAR TRILOGY
MYSTERIOUS TEMPLAR by Adriana Girolami
THE CRIMSON AMULET by Adriana Girolami
TEMPLAR'S REDEMPTION by Adriana Girolami

MYSTERY
BONE'S PARADOX by Buck Stienke
RECIPE for MURDER by Ken Farmer & Buck Stienke
SIN NO MORE by Ken Farmer & Buck Stienke
THE LOCK BOX by Terry D. Heflin
THREE CREEKS by Ken Farmer
RED HILL ROAD by Ken Farmer
THE POND by Ken Farmer

CIVIL WAR ESPIONAGE ROMANCE
SCARLET HEM by Terry D. Heflin
GOLDEN CIRCLE by Terry D. Heflin

Coming Soon
MYSTERY
FRIENDS by Ken Farmer

CIVIL WAR ESPIONAGE ROMANCE
THE AMETHYST by Terry D. Heflin

HISTORICAL FICTION WESTERN
McGRATH by T.C. Miller
DALIA MARRH by Ken Farmer

HISTORICAL FICTION ROMANCE
DAUGHTER of HADES by Adriana Girolami
ZAMINDAR and the LADY by Adriana Girolami

SY/FY
ANTAREAN DILEMMA by T.C. Miller

TIMBER CREEK PRESS